RECOVERY

Chris Boult

© Chris Boult 2015

All rights reserved

No part of this publication may be reproduced, stored in a retrieval system, or transmitted in any form or by any means, without the prior permission in writing of the publisher, nor be otherwise circulated in any form of binding or cover other than that in which it is published and without a similar condition including this condition being imposed on the subsequent purchaser.

First published in Great Britain

All paper used in the printing of this book has been made from wood grown in managed, sustainable forests.

ISBN: 978-1-78003-868-1

Printed and bound in the UK
Author Essentials
4 The Courtyard
Falmer
E. Sussex
BN1 9PQ

A catalogue record of this book is available from the British Library

Cover design by Jacqueline Abromeit

About the Author

Chris studied in Nottingham in the late 1970s, joined the TA and later the regular army before joining the probation service in 1986. He served as a probation officer and as a manager in various settings and at different levels, working mostly with high risk offenders and often closely with both the police and the prison service. He retired from service in 2015. He started writing novels in 2013 and this is his third book.

Other books by Chris Boult and some comments from reviews:

IN THE SHADOW OF THE BAYONET

'The story is a good read, quite a page turner.'

'More interesting than the whodunit novels in this genre.'

'The book explores themes of justice, political intrigue and civil-military relations with an international dimension.'

OUT OF THE SHADOW

'Chris's rich and varied life experiences enable him to write pacey tales with a strong central character.'

'Another triumph, looking forward to his next book.'

'It was brilliant, had my emotions going, an excellent follow on.'

Acknowledgements

Thanks to all involved in supporting and contributing to this venture and helping to bring this book to publication, with a special thanks to Ang, and all at Author Essentials for their patience and perseverance.

Dedicated to the victims of crime

'It's never too late to be what you might have been.'

                                                  T.S Eliot.

Preface

RECOVERY –
A Victim's Story

Victims have traditionally regarded their interests as being under-represented in the criminal justice system and many still do. This story is an attempt to reflect some of those feelings and air some of the underlying issues. It is a story about human tragedy, but most of all it is a story of hope and of RECOVERY.

The characters portrayed are not intended to resemble any specific individuals but simply to reflect and enhance the story.

Whilst the book is based on my experiences and knowledge of criminal justice, I have indulged in a degree of poetic licence.

As my third book, I hope that I am learning and improving with experience. I acknowledge that the first book, *In the Shadow of the Bayonet*, with hindsight was published in some haste and the proofreading and editing process was not as thorough as it should have been. I apologise for this. Feedback received from my first two books has inevitably been varied, but comments have been largely favourable, useful and encouraging, so thank you to all who have taken the trouble to tell me what you think or to write a review.

Finally, I would like to acknowledge the impact of crime in general on victims and hope that their plight does receive greater acknowledgement, consideration and agency attention.

GLOSSARY OF TERMS

CPN	Community Psychiatric Nurse
CPS	Crown Prosecution Service
DCI	Detective Chief Inspector
FLO	Police Family Liaison Officer
RECCE	Reconnaissance
SIO	Police Senior Investigating Officer
SNOUT	Police Informer

PART ONE

THE INCIDENT

Chapter One

'We've found her; she seems OK,' said the police officer with a mixture of excitement and relief. 'She's back in the underground car park from where she was abducted. She looks dazed and upset, but physically alright as far as I can see.'

'Excellent! Well done!' replied the operational commander. I'll let the parents know immediately... I don't suppose there's any sign of the perpetrator or any obvious evidence or leads?'

'No, sir, nothing obvious; looks like he's just brought her back and dumped her. I just hope he hasn't caused her any harm in the meantime.'

'Quite; so do I. Time will tell.'

For this two-year-old girl and her parents this was a lucky escape from tragedy. Unfortunately, in another place at about the same time, events were not going to turn out so well...

*

Jan Hartwell locked the outhouse and garage doors of their family home in Norfolk and returned to the house to make a hot drink. Her husband, Mark, was out at a farmer's union function that evening. Sam, their oldest son was at home, as was April, their only daughter, both choosing to spend their time alone in their bedrooms. It was a quiet and peaceful evening. Jan was downstairs and enjoyed these moments being on her own to be able to relax, to reflect, to unwind. They were a distraction from the normal pressures of life and a chance, she felt, to recharge her battery.

On the whole Jan felt quite satisfied with her life. She was proud of her family. They had experienced their difficulties, like most families, but the bonds between them remained strong. Tensions and differences had been dealt with over the years. Jan felt sad as she thought of friends whose families had separated and of the pain that it had caused. There was even a sense of smugness in her mind as she remembered family events and the good times. The thought crossed her mind that maybe this was wishful thinking. Was she allowing herself to contemplate through rose-tinted spectacles? She disregarded the thought.

It was cold for early winter and it had been raining heavily. Jan put another log on the fire and settled down on the sofa to read her favourite magazine. Her life in a rural community had in many ways sheltered her from some of the harsher aspects of humanity. She felt a sense of calm, tranquillity and security.

As it approached midnight, she thought of going to bed. There was no need to wait for Mark as she knew that he would be a while yet. Suddenly the silence of the evening and her peace and solitude were broken by flashing lights as a car approached at speed and turned onto her drive. As Jan went to take a look, four wet and bedraggled men got out of the car quickly and forced their way past her through the front door and into the house. The first man shot and killed the family dog with a crossbow as he started to bark. Jan opened the door into the living room in fear and disbelief trying to get away. She turned as she saw Sam coming down the staircase looking concerned, half asleep and confused, only to be met with a hail of heavy blows from baseball bats, rendering him battered, bruised and unconscious.

Quickly and efficiently the men spread out throughout the downstairs of the house. All were wearing surgical gloves. They searched Jan for mobile phones, questioned her where other mobiles would be in the house and disconnected the landline. They then demanded access to the barn to hide their car, the dead dog and the crossbow. Jan noticed that they didn't start collecting other valuable items from around the house and wondered why and what was actually happening. What was this? Who were these men and what did they want?

While they were searching, Jan managed to locate her mobile phone and quickly started to dial the police before she heard a firm voice from behind her.

'Drop it, bitch. Last warning, next time it'll hurt bad!'

She complied. She still didn't know what she was dealing with. Three phones were collected and duly smashed using the baseball bats, placed in a bag and stashed away.

'Look, I don't know who you are, or what you want, but this is my house you're intruding and that's my son laying on the floor. He needs help – you can't just ignore him!' Jan pleaded.

'Quiet, bitch. I'll tell you when to talk. Bind her!' he instructed one of the others. Quickly two men gagged Jan and tied her hands behind her back, sat her in a chair and tied her to it.

Jan went cold. What is this? If it's not a robbery...then what is it? Who are these men? They sound like they are from London, but one of the voices sounds more local, she thought, as a cold sense of terror and anxiety raced through her mind and body.

The four men moved away out of earshot.

'Right,' said Barry, the gang leader, 'phase one completed....now food. Remember to keep your gloves on at all times everyone.'

Chaff made himself useful in the kitchen with Dog while Barry and Charlie considered their next move.

'OK, Charlie, the paintings have been moved successfully, we've found a nice little hide away and now we wait. The house is off the beaten track and easy to defend; there's only one way in and out by vehicle, and approach across country would be visible in open ground like this. We need an all round observation point. Can you sort that after we've eaten?'

'Yes, sure, boss.'

'We need to make sure no one will be visiting for the next few days. A house this big might be busy and there are probably more family members unaccounted for. That could be tricky. I'll get that information from the bitch.'

'What about the boy, boss, do you think he'll be OK? We don't want to risk a murder charge,' posed Charlie.

'Um, you're right, we better check him – a job for Chaff.'

Chaff went across to the prostrate body and kicked it. The boy moaned. Alive, he judged, and that was good enough.

'So he's OK. Dog, did you finish searching the rest of the house?' responded Barry.

'No, boss.'

'Well get onto it. Charlie, go with him.'

Jan heard this and cringed, fearing the worst, before Chaff started to interrogate her about likely visitors to the house.

It was a large and spacious family home. Dog and Charlie started to search upstairs room by room, along corridors, checking cupboards. They weren't really sure what they were looking for, anything, they supposed. Dog went into a bathroom. He noticed that there were plenty of towels around and toothbrushes. Was this some sort of bed and breakfast? he wondered. They checked several bedrooms, all were empty and they checked what was some sort of storeroom, packed with various household items. Charlie went through a closed door into what was obviously a further bedroom, and Dog followed. They looked at each other.

'This smells occupied,' remarked Dog.

'Yes, it's been used for sure,' replied Charlie, checking round. He put his hand in the bed. 'This bed's warm, it's been slept in!'

Looking round the room, all the clues indicated female occupation. 'Where is she?' posed Dog, looking under the bed. Charlie looked behind furniture. They continued their search, expectant, intrigued, excited. Then he opened the wardrobe door to reveal a teenage girl standing shaking in silence, wearing only a long pink nightdress.

'What have we here, Dog?'

'Well, well, well; would you believe it? Looks like this job comes with its own entertainment.' April's shaking increased. They didn't notice, not seeing the person – paying her no heed.

Dog directed her out of the wardrobe. Hesitantly April stepped out onto the bedroom carpet and froze. She was fifteen years old, innocent, naive, inexperienced, gentle, kind, trusting and vulnerable. These precious things were all suddenly at risk.

The two men taunted April for a while, sensing her unease, her powerlessness and her vulnerability before they started to assault her. They had no thoughts of the consequences, the impact or the morality of their actions. Driven by opportunism, lust and a sense of reckless power and control they began pulling off her nightdress, lifting it from the bottom up and over her head to expose a surprisingly mature naked form. She froze as they directed her forward and positioned her on her back lying on the bed and Charlie took hold of a leg, holding it outwards, inviting Dog to have first go. Dog began to touch, to taste, to reveal, to intrude, to invade. Ignoring April's visible distress, Dog began to undress whilst Charlie hung onto her leg. April was too frightened to move, to fight to resist, or even to speak.

She had been asleep and had woken dreaming of a friend's birthday party that was coming up soon. The image included use of a barn, with a band and a bar and a barbeque on a warm summer's evening. Then she had become slightly unnerved by noise downstairs and wondered what was happening. Was it some people leaving the party in her dream? Was it cars arriving to collect them? She wasn't sure, but as she became more awake and the dream faded, she became increasingly convinced that this wasn't her imagination and that something was wrong. She had felt confused and didn't know what to do, so like a little girl she had pulled the covers over her head and rolled over, hoping if she ignored it that it would simply go away. Sadly, it didn't go away, as she had heard voices and men coming up the stairs. April had panicked and like a bad game of hide-and-seek had quickly looked for somewhere to escape being found. She had stepped into the wardrobe just before the men had entered her room.

Dog looked at his mate as if kindly offering to let him undress next, whilst he took over holding the leg; the least he could do for a mate, he thought. April was still frozen and still hadn't said a word. No words seemed adequate; what could she say? She knew they weren't listening. It felt like she wasn't really there. Whilst Charlie was getting ready, Dog moved towards her head, forcing himself into her mouth and demanding that she respond, stimulating him. April choked, but he persisted, tears forming in her eyes, but he didn't care. Sobs didn't distract him either as Charlie moved to lay over her and take away what little dignity she had had left. Once he had finished with her as if with the casual disregard of sharing a cigarette, Charlie got off and Dog got on, continuing the movement and the distress.

April tried not to look at them, but when she did she could see only coldness and bitterness. She could smell their bad breath and the incongruous medical smell of surgical gloves. She didn't understand. Why? Why her? Why here? Why now? It was too much to comprehend. Not for her the gentle voyage of sexual discovery with a chosen partner. Not for her the warmth and heat of emotion and the joy of satisfaction. No. For her only the feelings of desperation, distress, confusion, pain, disgust and anger.

They carried on and did it again – she felt helpless. Suddenly there was a distraction, a noise downstairs. A car had arrived; was it help? Was it a rescue? No, April could hear her father's voice as he came in singing, having returned from the farmer's union function. She glanced at her clock. It was one o'clock in the morning. Voices called for her two tormentors and grumbling they quickly dressed and left – left, leaving a young girl distraught, destroyed, never to be the same again. April looked down at her soiled and abused body and just cried.

Mark Hartwell was a strong-minded, independent man, who worked in the local farming community for an agricultural supplies firm. He walked into his house in a buoyant mood after a good evening. This was not what he was expecting to find. The atmosphere was tense, the house felt strange. Where were his family? Where was his dog to greet him? Before he could begin to answer his own questions Mark became aware of the presence of strangers.

'Who the hell are you buggers in my house?' he cried.

Dog approached him from behind and in a skilled and practiced move gripped him around the throat inducing unconsciousness.

'Good man,' said Barry as Mark fell to the ground. 'He's too drunk to be worth bothering with now; we'll deal with him in the morning. Just secure him and make sure he doesn't drown on his own vomit,' he ordered. Dog nodded.

Dog had removed Jan's gag ready for further questioning, when April appeared at the bottom of the stairs in her nightdress. There were tears on her face. Jan felt sick and was instantly overcome with feelings of dread, fear and anger.

'April, April darling!' she cried. Staring at the intruders she demanded, 'What have you done to her? What have you done?' whilst fearing that she knew – and looking into April's eyes only confirmed her worst fears.

April ran to her, hugging her mother who was still tied to the chair as she continued to cry. Many more tears would follow.

Chapter Two

The gang had targeted a large multinational pharmaceuticals company located just north of London, that they knew from an inside source held a substantial art collection. During the economic downturn, companies who lacked the business confidence to invest had sometimes turned to art and similar commodities to secure their assets, as more conservative forms of investment often gave such minimal returns. As well as providing a more balanced investment portfolio for such firms, it also opened up new avenues of opportunity for criminal gangs. Cash, the gang reasoned, could more easily be traced these days but art could be high value and was portable and readily saleable, through the right channels, of course.

The raid had all gone without a hitch. The inside man's information proved to be correct, and the gang had turned up at the offices two hours before the legitimate removals firm was booked to conduct the office move. They explained that they had a cancellation and so their schedules had changed, whilst they loaded all the requisite furniture, together with the removal of the art work and left just before the real firm had arrived.

After the initial confusion following the arrival of the second removal van, it took some time before anyone thought of theft – a simple misunderstanding seemed the likely explanation, as the office move had been ordered, planned and arranged by staff from a distant head office. It wasn't until someone actually checked with head office and then checked around to see if anything else was missing that the art theft was discovered.

Known only to a select few staff there was also a small collection of gold bars stored in the same place, which the gang had discovered whilst carefully removing the paintings. They couldn't believe their luck as they discovered this added bonus. So by the time the alarm was raised and the police became involved, the gang were long gone. The furniture remained in the van, parked on a large lorry park by a transport café, where it had attracted no attention. The art and the gold had been transferred to another vehicle for onward transmission via various means, through various hands to pre-arranged art dealers keen to sell the paintings on, mostly to connections in China and Russia.

The gang had transferred to a third vehicle further along the route, leaving the art work and the gold to continue their journey. They had then headed to the pre-arranged rural retreat where the unsuspecting Hartwell family had been subjected to their uninvited intrusion.

*

'Who else lives in this house or might be visiting over the next few days, bitch?' demanded Chaff of Jan Hartwell.

Jan was still thinking of the telling look in her daughter's eyes as she struggled to respond, before a fist hit her hard in the ribs.

'Come on, come on; we're not pissing about here!'

'No one else lives here!' Jan cried out, whilst nursing her battered side. 'There was no need for that.'

'Listen, honey, we'll do what we want, as you saw with that little tart of a daughter of yours,' he said, whilst approaching her to stroke her hair. 'You never know, you may get lucky; we may try you next!' he taunted.

Jan just cringed, froze and felt physically sick at even the thought. Then another blow struck.

'Now, who else will be coming?'

'I don't know! I'm not expecting anyone, but people do call,' Jan replied in tears.

'Not good enough. Who? Who?' demanded Chaff again.

'Neighbours; delivery people; I don't know...oh, and Margaret, our cleaner...on Thursdays.'

'No one and now Margaret! You'd better be telling me the truth, bitch!' he insisted as he twisted her arm.

'What would you know of truth?' she replied defiantly.

'Don't get smart with me, bitch. Right, ring Margaret and cancel, and ring the neighbours and tell them all to stay away as the whole family's got flu.'

As Jan began to follow his instructions she felt cold. It was only Tuesday, did they really intend to stay as long as Thursday? She was horrified at the thought. This was awful; this was intolerable. This was inhumane, well beyond anything that she had experienced before. These men just acted as they liked with no heed for anyone. How will it end? she thought. Will it end? Jan was incensed but could read a glance and anticipated a blow. She made the call.

Margaret received the call and thought it was rather odd. In thirty years she couldn't remember the Hartwell family ever cancelling, but didn't dwell on it. The neighbours reacted differently, with some simply grateful to be forewarned and others keen to offer help to fetch shopping or call the doctors, or whatever they could do. With Chaff standing ominously over her, Jan had dealt with their concerns, rejecting all offers of help.

Under threat she then rang her husband and son's employers and her daughter's school to inform them of their respective non-attendance due to flu. She just hoped desperately that someone would be able to read between the lines, sense that things were not as she described and react. She desperately longed for help, any help; anything to bring this nightmare to an end.

The school secretary did think it was a little strange with no other reports of flu, and Mark's colleagues from his firm that supplied animal feedstuff to the local economy were more amused than concerned.

'What? Flu? Flu? So what?' said one of his mates.

'You wait till we tell the blokes in the pub this one! Bloody flu!' responded another.

'Shouldn't be any problem with unexpected visitors, boss,' Chaff reported back to Barry.

'Good,' he replied.

'How much longer we staying here then, boss?' asked Chaff.

Barry responded that he had no plans to move yet.

While sitting in the kitchen they had heard reports on the radio news of their theft of the art collection. The kitchen had become their sort of base. They had smashed the television to deny the family access to any news. The gold had not been mentioned. A comprehensive search had been launched and the furniture van had been found, but police reported no leads on who may have been responsible. A spokesman anticipated that whoever had committed this serious crime had probably crossed the Channel from one of the southern ports in the time before the alarm was raised. Questions were asked in parliament about the safety of business assets and personal property and the minister had given his personal assurance that every effort would be made to catch these men, bring them to justice and recover the property.

By midday Tuesday the family were starting to feel hungry having only been fed a few snacks. The gang had occupied the kitchen and set about eating their way through the contents of the fridge and the freezer, leaving a terrible mess. They had also drunk all they could find in the beer cupboard and had stolen all the bottles from the cabinet in the dining room. This included Mark's collection of fine malt whiskey and several special bottles of wine that Sam had brought back from his last trip to France and they were glugging them back as if they were cheap lager.

By this time the family were all contained in the living room with only their arms bound. Mark was awake and contending with the combination of a hangover, a bang to the head as he had fallen and the dawning realisation of what was happening. Jan hadn't said anything to him about what she suspected had happened to April; it was too painful and she feared that Mark would not be able to contain his anger and that they may all suffer as a consequence. Better to keep quiet, at least for now, she thought. Sam had also started to come round. He reported feeling sick and was quite confused. April was still asleep on the sofa. Jan contained herself, drew a deep breath and went to approach the men.

She walked cautiously towards the kitchen. It suddenly occurred to her for the first time that she could at least observe what these men looked like, which may help in the future – if there was to be a future. She noticed all had long hair and some combination of beard and moustache. She estimated that they were all mid-twenties, early thirties and white, although the one they called Chaff looked mixed race.

'Where do you think you're going, bitch?' shouted Charlie as Jan approached the kitchen door.

'I realise you don't give a toss for the needs of my family, but I do, and my son needs medical attention and we all need to eat,' she said firmly.

'Feeding time at the zoo!' scoffed Charlie.

'Yes throw a few crumbs in their direction!' replied Dog.

'They may even do some tricks!' laughed Chaff.

'OK,' said Barry, 'Charlie fix them some food and give them some water. As regards your son, there's no chance of medical attention, so do what you can to help him yourselves.'

'You gave him a bad head injury, remember? He'll need monitoring and some form of professional assessment. He also feels sick.'

'Just keep him alive. Give her some aspirin, Dog,' was the curt and callous response.

Chapter Three

The police investigation was only hitting dead ends. No witness reports of any value had emerged, no information was forthcoming from the criminal fraternity and there was no trace of the stolen goods. Forensic information was still coming in, but early indications weren't promising.

'There must be something!' exclaimed Chief Inspector Natalie Goodwin to her team as they all gathered for a briefing and review of the evidence. 'These people always leave some trace. We just have to find it. Who knew about the paintings? Was there inside information? Who's missing from their local patch? Who's suddenly looking good and spending lots of money? Come on folks, we need a lead. I've got the chief superintendent on my back and the local MP is making a lot of noise!'

'Not a pretty sight... Have you seen the chief super?'

'Isn't that what MPs do?'

'This isn't going to get our Natalie her next promotion, is it?' were just a range of thoughts and whispered comments from the audience.

'So, Sergeant Pickles, please take us through what we *do* know.'

'Yes, ma'am,' replied the keen young sergeant, referring to the incident board.

'We know that four men all aged mid to late twenties arrived at the pharmaceuticals company at 10 o'clock on Monday morning. Three of the men have been consistently identified as white, probably British, and one as black from Afro Caribbean origin and again probably British. All have been described as having long hair with a moustache and or beard. Precise descriptions vary.

'We know that they dressed and appeared like the legitimate removal firm and were well briefed, probably by an insider who is yet to be identified. They were all described as very helpful and courteous in their manner. They were shown where the furniture was and simply left to get on with it, stealing the paintings as they cleared the office. The inventory does not appear to be entirely comprehensive or up to date, but the firm believe that six paintings are missing, all by different artists. They are conservatively estimated to be worth two to three million pounds on the open market, so about half of that to the gang, depending on how many times they change hands before sale. Our art boys tell me that paintings such as these will sell easily in certain parts of the world, with no questions asked and probably be stored as investments rather than displayed anywhere.

'The gang then moved to the transport café/lorry park to unload and change vehicles. This attracted no attention and there was no CCTV so we don't know at this stage what vehicle or vehicles they may have left in. The timings indicate sufficient time to be well away before we were contacted, via almost any of the southern ports or airports. So they have had it easy folks. Now we must make it hard for them.

'So, Isaac, I want you and your team to concentrate on ports. Eleanor, your team on airports and Gavin yours on road transport. Usual form; ask the known players, check with security for your allotted task, anything suspicious, *anything*; bring it back to this meeting. OK? Questions? No? Right, go!'

'They must have gone to the ports and by ferry, so easy to mingle and become 'invisible', all going to separate ports if they had any sense,' said the DCI.

'Does that suggest the paintings are destined for sale in mainland Europe then...?' replied Sergeant Pickles, trying to impress.

'Yes, good thinking; you may well be right!'

Meanwhile a contact was waiting to receive the stolen goods and to proceed to the next stage of their journey.

'How much longer will we have to wait? When are they going to arrive?' demanded Herman. 'They should be in contact by now!'

'Steady, Herman; lots of things can cause delay – there's no need to panic yet,' replied his accomplice.

Herman was impatient to get on with it. Time scales were tight and further complicated by different international time zones. There wasn't much margin for error if the bounty was to get to its destination and achieve a premium price quickly. Barry was primarily a thief, not a distributor. He had to trust his contacts to arrange that, for a sizable cut, of course, but this time with the added value of the gold there was plenty of money for everyone. Herman was experienced in such matters and had carefully built up a large circle of contacts to enable the sale of 'acquired' property quickly. Speed was the key, before the authorities could trace their movements. He prided himself, with typical German efficiency, to be at least two steps ahead of the game at all times, and generally he was.

This sale was going to be one of his best. Six high value and rare paintings would always attract interest from professional collectors more interested in art than any notions of legitimate ownership. The Russian and Chinese markets were vast and still largely secret societies. Once sold, Western authorities realistically would have very little chance of recovery, he reasoned. So the key was to move the goods quickly out of Europe, but Herman was still waiting.

Chapter Four

Pascal was ready to leave, as agreed. He called into Henry's office before he went.

'Well, Henry, a job well done, it seems!'

'Yes, the police are clueless!' he responded. 'So you are ready to go and everything is in place. Well good luck, Pascal, and it's been good working with you,' he said as the two men shook hands.

Pascal left with his painting already dispatched to an address in northern Spain. He was to travel home to France initially then settle in Spain with the proceeds. Pascal had been careful to tell Henry only about his French connections. Although he trusted him, he preferred to keep his options open.

Pascal had worked for the firm for three years and had done well, but he had independent ambitions. He was the insider who had helped the gang identify and steal the paintings. Henry had encouraged him, knowing that he had destroyed the official inventories himself and could secure a valuable painting of his own to supplement his pension. He had agreed with Pascal to take one additional painting each and blame their loss on the gang. Henry had in fact taken two. In the North London office only he had been aware of the gold bars. They were 'unofficial' and had been acquired during some dubious pharmaceutical drugs dealings in Central Africa. Only one senior manager in head office was aware of their existence in his office vault, as far as he knew. They were gone in any event, and as they didn't officially exist and had never been declared for tax purposes. Henry and his associate could hardly cry foul now! Neither could they disclose their theft to the police, as they didn't 'exist'. For the company it was an embarrassing and very expensive loss.

Henry Stewart-Montague was ready to retire. He had worked hard for the firm and felt that he owed them nothing. This final chapter would no doubt blot his copy book, but he hoped to ride that and leave without any suspicion. If needs be he had already decided that he was prepared to sacrifice Pascal to save himself. Henry felt that after all he had no loyalty to Pascal. He reasoned that he was never likely to see him again and could get away with it using charm, connections and subterfuge.

*

In the house, the food had gone down well with all the family as time approached mid-afternoon on Tuesday.
April was very withdrawn, and Sam still felt quite confused. Jan was just holding it together but Mark was now alert and in tune with what was going on and he didn't like it – he didn't like it one bit! How dare these men just walk into their home, into their lives and act as if they owned the place and them with it! He was angry, but was trying to stay in control, whilst also thinking of an escape plan.

There was a knock on the front door. Everyone froze. Barry responded quickly. Referring to Jan, he said, 'Just answer the door calmly. I'll be right behind you. Tell whoever it is that the family have flu and they should stay away.' He untied her arms.

Jan nodded and went to the door slowly, trying to be calm and convincing. Could she dare give any form of signal? As she opened the door just enough to see, leaving it on the chain, it was a neighbour who greeted her.

'Hi Jan, just wondered if you were all alright; the house seemed very quiet and inactive. Just wondered if I could help?'

'No, but thanks anyway. We all have the flu; best stay away. Bye.' And she shut the door. She could sense Barry close behind her and hadn't dared try to deviate from his instructions. He seemed satisfied. She wondered whether she had managed to convey any sense of disquiet.

'Who was it, Barry?' Dog enquired.

'Just a neighbour; it's OK,' he replied.

Jenny left feeling a little uneasy. She shared her concerns with her husband, but they decided not to interfere.

At the agricultural suppliers, Mark's mates were surprised not to have heard from him personally by Tuesday afternoon as he was usually so conscientious.

'Where's that skiving bastard?' said one colleague, sympathetically.

'Yes, this isn't like Mark, we're busy and we need him here.' said one of the others. 'I'm going that way later, I'll call round and kick his arse.'

The others agreed, whilst Mavis, the unit secretary suggested taking some fruit and the others were thinking more of returning his P45.

Back at the farmhouse Dog and Chaff were beginning to get restless. They were starting to feel edgy. Had they already stayed too long?

Confined to the living room, Mark wondered how long it would take the gang to notice his absence if he did manage to slip out and try to fetch help. They did seem quite distracted. Jan sat on the sofa with April and just held her, her arms having not been retied. April could feel her warmth and concern without the need for words. Whatever happens, will she ever get over this? Jan wondered.

Barry was starting to think of a night move and was thinking of tonight.

*

DCI Goodwin paced up and down waiting for reports back from her officers. She was young, keen and ambitious. Her partner, Hayley, was a CPS prosecutor. Together they made a formidable pair. Over the years their relationship had raised some eyebrows, but attitudes were changing, albeit slowly.

Sergeant Andy Pickles walked in with some news. 'I've had reports back now from all the officers and there's nothing to collaborate, suggest, or cast suspicion of a move through the southern ports.'

'Um,' she responded, 'it seems we were wrong then, or could we have missed them? We need to widen the search. Andy, redeploy the teams to enquire further afield; I'm going back to the pharmaceutical company offices to have another look there.'

'OK, ma'am, one of the lads will be available to come with you.'

'Really,' she said.

Natalie left alone and drove to the office. She was beginning to think that this raid had gone all too smoothly. She wanted to talk to Henry Stewart-Montague.

'Ah, Chief Inspector, how kind of you to call,' said Henry, greeting her at reception.

'Mr Stewart-Montague, I just wanted to go over a few things with you again.'

'Sure, be my guest.'

Over enthusiasm and eagerness to please were often indications of something to hide, Natalie reflected as they walked through the office.

'Can we start with the vaults, please, sir? How many people would have known about the existence of the paintings? And why hold paintings? And why here, Mr Stewart-Montague?'

'Henry, please. Not many, for obvious reasons. Only I and a handful of the more senior staff knew of the paintings. As to why; well, art is a more secure investment than holding capital these days. Why here? Simply because we happened to have a vault.'

'Please let me have a list of names, Henry,' she replied. 'Do you have any concerns about the honesty of any of your staff?'

'No, of course not!'

'It occurs to me that this job all went so smoothly that it may have been difficult to achieve without some inside help.'

'You mean one of my employees may have been part of the gang?'

'I didn't say that, Henry. Is that what you think?'

'Well, well, no...' replied Henry, blustering.

'Come on Henry, a criminal gang arrive precisely two hours before your appointed removal firm and apparently know where the paintings are stored and manage to remove – did you say six of them – and the furniture, without a hitch and without anyone noticing anything wrong?'

'Err, err, it was nine paintings actually!'

'Nine now? How come the difference?'

'Well, as I said, our records weren't too good and I've since found a more recent inventory.'

'So your firm holds a considerable amount of its assets in the form of high value art and no one is accountable for keeping an accurate inventory. Henry, come on!' challenged Natalie, sensing an opening.

Henry blustered some more, but was less than convincing. The DCI interviewed some other staff before she left leaving Henry in no doubt that serious questions remained.

As she drove back to the station she reflected how such an apparent blustering idiot had reached such a senior position as the local manager in such a prominent company. Natalie felt sure that there had been inside involvement and that Henry knew about it. Also his name – Henry Stewart-Montague – is a little flamboyant, she thought. Is it genuine?

Mark's work mate was driving to see a customer and planned to call in to see Mark on the way. As he approached he did think it was odd that they hadn't heard from him. Despite the ribbing he had received in the office, Mark was well thought of, reliable and hard working. This just wasn't like him. George pulled into the drive and felt quite unnerved. He sensed that something wasn't right. He got out of his car and stood just watching the house for a moment. Two things struck him: where was Mark's car, and as it was Tuesday late afternoon, why weren't the bins out for collection in the morning? He walked round the large drive area. The barn at the back of the property was usually open, but today it was closed. It also struck him as odd that the family dog hadn't barked. Then, glancing across at the house, George was sure that he saw a strange man in the house through the side window. Now he really was alarmed. He decided not to knock on the door, but returned to his car quickly and drove off.

Instinct told him to act. George pulled over into a lay-by and called the police.

'This may sound odd, but I'm concerned about a work mate and have just been to his house. Something doesn't add up and I'm sure I saw a strange man in their house. Am I getting carried away or could this be serious?' posed George.

'Could you describe the man, sir?' asked the police control centre.

'It was only a fleeting glance but I think he had long hair, and I think a beard...'

The message was quickly passed to Sergeant Pickles

'Something's come in, ma'am,' he said to his DCI. 'There's been a report of a car driving fast and erratically in that area on the day of the raid and a report of a man missing from work who lives in a relatively isolated farmhouse, about thirty miles from the incident. A friend visited, felt it was odd and thought he saw a stranger in the house...with long hair and a beard...'

*

Sergeant Pickles and his DCI considered this latest development.

'Andy, a few things strike me. Firstly, if this is the same gang and there's a link between the art theft and the concerns about the Hartwell family, is this where the gang went to? If so, why this house and why did it take them so long to get there? In other words, was the selection of the Hartwells' house really random, or preselected, and if so, why? Also, what happened between leaving the site of the theft at about 12 o'clock and arriving at the Hartwells', which we think was some time after dark?'

'Yes, ma'am, if the house was already set as the target to hide out, why that particular house? Was it just the convenience of the short distance from the pharmaceutical firm, or is there something else? Then you're right, why take so long to travel thirty miles to get there?'

Together with her suspicions about Henry, Natalie thought that this was enough to justify action, and time wasn't on their side. The priority was to secure the farmhouse. 'Right, get together a large enough force to surround the property, including a firearms team. The gang might have been that close to us all along. Also, we need to know who normally occupies the house. We know how many are in the gang, but we don't know the total number of people held in what now looks like a hostage situation and that could be critical. Come on Andy, we're going in!' said Natalie, getting excited. She loved the adrenalin rush where operations were concerned, and had been commended several times for swift and decisive action, putting her own safety at risk to secure an arrest.

Chapter Five

Sam had been sick several times during the afternoon and was clearly in some difficulty. April was crying to see her brother suffering so badly. Mark was boiling and Jan was just trying to keep it together. The stress of the situation and their unusual close proximity was taking its toll. Latent tensions were becoming apparent. Jan was trying desperately to be the conciliator but she was struggling.

Some basic provisions were starting to run out, and the urine bucket in the corner and the blood stains from the hall meant that the house smelt and the atmosphere was becoming increasingly unpleasant. Both the family and the gang were wondering how long they could sustain this arrangement. For the gang, it was a question of how long they needed to; for the family there didn't seem any choice.

Barry was also beginning to struggle to hold his boys in check. Dog was all for making a move and Chaff had other thoughts on his mind concerning April. Charlie thought that confinement to the living room was not enough and that they needed to tie the family up more firmly and secure them before things got out of hand.

Barry decided he had to do something, so called his boys into the kitchen.

'Boys, maybe we've overstayed our welcome. I think it's time to prepare to go. The indications are that the police are still clueless but think that we have already escaped across the Channel, so we have achieved what we set out to by being here. Driving south to the lorry park and then doubling back north after we'd offloaded the goods seems to have worked as a deception plan. While we were north of the incident they looked south and they are not going to be looking around here if we move now. So Dog, try to calm the family and make sure that they stay in the one room. I'm going to fuel up the car then we'll go after dark, OK?' The others all agreed and were both relieved and happy with the plan.

So was Mark who had heard enough to be aware of their intentions. Taking advantage of the gang's temporary withdrawal from the living room and lax security, Mark had moved as close to the kitchen as he dared. He had managed to hear the gist of the gang's conversation. Having done so he was feeling pleased with his efforts while he returned to the living room and mulled over what actions he might take.

Charlie and Chaff were sharing thoughts on what they would spend their money on – fast cars, women and booze. Dog gave some thought to the exit plan. It was nice and simple; they had been careful not to leave any prints and had nothing to carry with them.

Barry left and drove the car out of its hiding place in the barn to find a petrol station. Jenny, the neighbour saw him drive away. How strange, she thought, the barn door opened and a car drove out but it wasn't any of the family's cars. This time she wondered whether she should report it to the local police or not.

Barry pulled into the nearest petrol station and filled up.

'Quiet, isn't it mate?' he commented to the kiosk attendant.

'You wouldn't have said that about fifteen minutes ago. Half the local police force seemed to call in for fuel;

dogs, firearms the lot! It used to be quiet round here, but you don't know these days!'

Barry felt a sense of panic, paid and rang Dog immediately. He couldn't get through and left a message on his answer phone telling him it was time to move and to meet him over the footbridge at the back of the track leading away from the house as it met the road. As he drove off he thought, why isn't he listening to his phone? Why do I bother with such idiots? Oh fuck it, I'll save myself, he decided as he headed east towards the coast in the hope of crossing the Channel and getting away alone. He pulled off his wig and all the fake facial hair to reveal a bald head and an almost clean-shaven face, but left his surgical gloves on whilst still in the car.

Jenny finally decided to ring 101 to report her concerns to the local police.

'Hello, I'm a neighbour of the Hartwell family in the village and have just seen something unusual.' Jenny reported calling at the house, feeling uneasy but not wanting to interfere, then seeing the strange car drive out of the barn.

'Can you describe the car, madam?'

'Oh yes! It was quite a big one!' replied Jenny.

'Did you notice the make or model, madam?'

'Oh no, I don't do cars, my husband does all that; he would know.'

'Well then can *he* tell me what make, model or colour it was?'

'Oh, no.'

'Why not, madam?'

'Because he didn't see it, but it was a sort of a large family type car, officer.'

'OK, madam. Thanks for your help.'

*

'Another report, ma'am; control have had a neighbour on the phone saying she's just seen an unknown car drive out of the Hartwell family barn, no details, but could it be them or some of them?'

'OK, thanks. I think we are onto something. It's been on the news again. Any more information from the public, Andy?'

Andy was used to the mixture of responses normally received in these circumstances from cranks and busybodies, the deluded and the lonely, all claiming to know the culprit. These were normal, but somewhere in the sea of information he knew there would be something useful. 'Mixed messages inevitably, ma'am, but Isaac's team did get a call from one of his snouts saying word was that a Barry from East London was heard to have been recruiting a gang and hasn't been seen around for a few days. Isaac did some digging and has come up with the name Barry Stoker. Stoker has form for being a planner, for armed robbery in his younger days and for theft involving large amounts of money. He could be our man. There's no trace on the car as yet.'

'Excellent! You've circulated his details to all forces, ports and airports and what little descriptions we have?'

'Yes, ma'am.'

'Good. Well done. Right, we now need to close in on the house and get these guys, hopefully without harming the family. You mentioned Stoker and armed robbery; what's the feeling about whether these boys are armed or not?'

'Don't really know, ma'am. Stoker hasn't got a lot of form for firearms, so it's an unknown.'

'Do we know the names of the others and whether they do firearms, Andy?'

'No, ma'am. We only know there were four men who lifted the paintings.'

'OK, so we have to assume they will be armed. How close are the officers now?'

'We can hear the commander on the ground live, ma'am. We have dogs in position on standby, a hostage negotiator ready and a firearms team approaching from the front and back of the house.'

In the house, tensions were mounting. April was restless and had asked to go for a shower. She just wanted to wash it all away – the thought, the smell, the horror. Without Barry the others were losing control of the situation. Whilst the three remaining men were agitated Mark considered whether this was his chance to make a run for it to get help. He couldn't easily share his thoughts with Jan while Dog was in the room so kept silent.

April went for her shower and Chaff followed her upstairs. He told her that Barry had said not to let any of them out of their sight and insisted on sitting in the bathroom to watch her. After the previous indignities April didn't particularly react, she just looked straight through him.

Mark took his chance as Dog followed Chaff upstairs. He asked to go to the toilet and went quickly through the back door using his own key and out into the garden. He reckoned he could make it cross country hidden from view behind the big hedge over to John, his neighbour on the left, raise the alarm and get back before Charlie had noticed. He set off in earnest, determined to try to rescue his family. It was very dark with heavy cloud and no moonlight as he stumbled into the night.

As April came out of the shower wrapped only in a towel, Chaff and Dog followed her into her bedroom. As she walked past and Dog closed the door behind them, Chaff just held the towel enough for it to drop to the ground leaving her standing naked before them. April suspected she knew what was coming next and felt numb. She couldn't quite regard these animals as real men. She couldn't see them as people and just felt cold and detached. She tried to take her mind elsewhere. How could these animals just take what they wanted without any regard? How could they keep her brother here knowing that he was dangerously ill? How could she defend herself? She felt helpless, with no choice but to allow it to happen.

Chaff and Dog started to sexually assault her – Dog holding, Chaff doing, as he felt it was his turn. Dog was goading her, ridiculing her and taunting her whilst Chaff abused her. She felt utterly powerless. She felt like an object, and somehow she felt strangely guilty as if it was her fault. She felt embarrassed for her family; she felt sad, but mostly she felt pain.

Hearing the soft sound of sobbing, Sam reacted, pushing Charlie away enough to run upstairs and burst into his sister's room. He had managed to untie his hands and threw a mighty haymaker of a punch at Dog who was still holding his sister's leg. Dog floundered. Charlie and Jan both ran in, too, and the room immediately became embroiled in a mad scramble for dominance, for survival, for dignity.

Outside, Mark had run into the approaching police officers on his way back to the building, and hearing the commotion had to be restrained to prevent him from re-entering the house.

Inside, the mayhem was disturbed by the sound of the loudspeaker.

'This is the police. We have the property surrounded. There is no escape. Let the hostages go and come out slowly one at a time,' instructed the officer calmly.

Dog and Chaff scrambled for clothing and pushed their way out of the bedroom. There was a doorway downstairs that led to the back of the house, into a utility area with an exit just a few yards from the side door of the barn. They made for that. Dog and Charlie ran first, but Chaff had second thoughts. He hadn't finished with April and he wanted more.

Jan and Sam sensed an opportunity to escape and staggered downstairs shouting to April to follow them. They were terrified and felt they needed to move quickly. Sam felt so sick and dizzy he thought he was about to collapse. They could hear the police calling them from outside as they stumbled out into the cold, dark night air. As they looked back April wasn't behind them but was still upstairs recovering what dignity she could muster to follow them, but before she could leave her room Chaff had doubled back into the house. Seeing Jan and Sam step out into the darkness he managed to slam and lock the front door and run upstairs blocking April's exit. Chaff forced her back into her bedroom, ordering her to remove the clothing she had just retrieved. He had a knife. He judged that the other two would inevitably get caught if the police were here in strength, but that with April, he may be able to talk his way out of this.

He raped her again at knifepoint on her bed, while the police were trying to establish what had happened and were reassessing the situation. The nightmare wasn't over. In fact it was far from over.

Outside, Jan sought the comfort of Mark's arms conveying her desperate concerns for April, whilst a doctor quickly examined Sam who by now was in a quite desperate condition. She was then ushered promptly into the back of an ambulance with her son to set off to the sanctuary and safety of a hospital before she realised that April hadn't managed to leave the house. Mark waved them off before waiting anxiously for news of April. Jan hadn't been able to tell him what had happened, but he'd guessed from her demeanour, and fearing for her safety wished desperately that April had managed to escape with Jan and Sam.

Dog and Charlie left the back of the barn and managed to creep away from the officers, down the track that Barry had mentioned on his answer phone message. It was pitch black as they staggered through the mud and puddles towards the footbridge and the road, and hopefully to meet Barry with the car, they thought.

Barry was in fact long gone. He had dumped his car and hired a Land Rover using a false identity and was still heading towards the coast wearing a wax jacket, green wellies and a tweed cap. As Dog and Charlie found the footbridge and began to cross it, suddenly they could see police with cars and dogs waiting for them.

'The bastard, he's double crossed us!' shouted Charlie.

'Looks like it, unless they've already got him,' replied Dog, as officers appeared at both ends of the narrow bridge. Although both men could swim, the prospect of jumping into icy cold water and probably still getting caught was not appealing. They were done. They had been caught.

Outside the house by now a whole army of emergency vehicles were present, lights had been erected and various plans were being formed to enter the building if necessary. At least there was no suggestion now that firearms were involved, but the threat of a knife spotted by Jan was a new and worrying dimension. The officer with the loudspeaker tried again to send a message to Chaff inside, whilst the commander on the ground consulted the hostage negotiator.

In the bedroom, Chaff drew back the curtains, opened the window and shouted out, 'The house is wired; I can set it alight at anytime! Stay back! You'll never take either of us alive!' April had thought of that possibility, and at that moment death could almost feel welcome.

'Did you see any wiring, Mark?' asked the police commander.

'No. He's bluffing. Don't let that bastard harm my daughter anymore. If you lot of spineless idiots with this whole army around you won't go in, then I will!'

'Mark, I understand your feelings, but that won't be necessary, sir.'

'I don't think you do. That's my daughter in there with him! She's in her bedroom having just come out of the shower. I don't think you need me to explain what is likely to be happening!' exclaimed Mark in desperation.

'No, sir, but we have to be careful not to make matters worse. I assure you I'll send my men in as soon as I think the risk to your daughter allows us to do so...but not until.'

Chaff pulled the curtain back across the window and turned to April for more. For the first time she opted to talk.

'Why?' she asked calmly.

'What do you mean, why, you little bitch?' replied Chaff gruffly.

'Why are you doing this?' April asked again.

'Killing time and coz I want to!'

'Has it occurred to you that I might not?'

'Shut up you silly tart!' he said angrily as he slapped her hard across the face and threatened her with the knife to keep quiet.

Outside, one of the officers was taking details from Mark to try to assess the level of threat posed to April, trying to establish Chaff's character and likely response, together with the commander, the hostage negotiator, the firearms team leader and the senior fire officer. Natalie, back in the control room had been unable to identify Chaff from the little they knew and couldn't help build the picture.

'So it looks like this guy is a new player?' suggested one of the officers.

'Or one that's not been caught yet!' posed the negotiator. 'We can't assume anything. What we know is that one man, armed with a knife is holding hostage a naked fifteen-year-old girl in that front bedroom up there. I don't buy his threats about wiring the house, but that doesn't mean he couldn't or wouldn't set it alight. I guess he reckons his mates didn't get away and so is desperate himself. In a sense he has nothing to lose. We need to persuade him that he does. Appeal to self interest – I doubt that any appeal for the interests of the girl will make any impact.'

'OK,' responded the police commander as competing thoughts flashed through his head of his moral and legal responsibilities and the potential risk of harming April. 'Gary, this is difficult for you firearms boys, in the dark with a target obscured in a building and little chance to engage him, at least as yet, so have your men stand by in case he tries to come out and use her as a shield. If he does that and threatens her with the knife, then that's good enough for me and you have my authority to shoot him. If I send you into the house then that's a completely different ball game and you'll have to respond to the situation as it appears, as you've been trained to do. However, we'll only do that as a last resort, because once he knows you're in, he could kill her before you get to him.

'For you fire and ambulance crews, it's a waiting game, I'm afraid; just be prepared to react while we try the softly softly approach first and see if we can talk him out.

'OK, Jack, it's over to you,' he said, as he turned to the hostage negotiator.

In the bedroom Chaff had assaulted April again. She had become really distressed, but he didn't care, he just kept abusing her. April was feeling desperate. She didn't have any idea of the preparations outside or of what Chaff was thinking or planning to do next. She felt very alone. She noticed that she was bleeding. The room smelt horrible. It had been her sanctuary, her private place, and now all that was gone. It felt like *his* territory, like *his* ground – and she wanted it back. She felt confused, violated, used, dirty, angry, guilty and sad all at the same time. But most of all she felt very scared.

As Chaff climbed off her, he turned away to wipe himself on her dressing gown and momentarily put the knife down on the side of the bed. April saw her chance, and leaning forward and taking the knife, she plunged the five inch blade into his side. She struck him in the area of his kidneys and as he reeled backwards April quickly jumped off the bed and ran out of the room, grabbing her towel as she went, and headed for the front door. Chaff was powerless to stop her.

Dressed in only a towel and still holding the bloodstained knife in her hand, April Hartwell emerged from the house into the mass of people outside. She was dazzled by the lights and overwhelmed by the reception as her father ran forward to meet her, to embrace her, to reassure her, and to make her feel safe.

Chapter Six

Once the naked, bleeding Chaff wearing only handcuffs and surgical gloves was arrested and taken from the house, the clean up started and the investigation could proceed.

For the family, although they would be forgiven for thinking the nightmare was over, sadly they were to discover that in many ways it had only just begun.

Sam was checked out at the hospital and found to have suffered concussion as suspected, as well as some colourful cuts and bruises; no bones were broken however. He was still woozy, having headaches and feeling sick. The medical team considered placing him in a medically induced coma and kept him in for observation and further tests.

Jan and Mark were treated initially for shock and trauma but displayed no further symptoms.

April, however, was in a very poor state. She had found the treatment of a rape victim to be almost as bad as the incident itself. By the time Jan was released from caring for Sam and had traced her daughter to the local police station it was nearly all over. She arrived at the desk anxious to intervene.

'Hi, I'm Jan Hartwell, mother of April Hartwell. My family has been the subject of what I suppose you would call a hostage situation, during which my daughter was raped and I understand that she is here now and I want to see her please,' Jan asked firmly.

'I don't think that will be necessary, madam,' replied the civilian receptionist, 'I think she has been dealt with.'

'Dealt with? She's just been raped for God's sake and she's only fifteen years old, technically a child! She needs her mother! Couldn't you have waited?'

'The doctor is very busy, madam and your husband has been present – ah, here she is now. I believe you are free to go.'

April emerged from a side door looking terrible. She looked distant and frozen. 'Darling, darling what have they done to you?'

April was too traumatised to answer and just stood there in a paper tracksuit, holding her wet towel, which was all she had. With nothing forthcoming from April Jan demanded to see someone in authority before Mark emerged from the toilet. After some time DCI Natalie Goodwin did come down to see the family and to apologise. After describing events, Mark decided April had gone through enough and set off to take her home while Jan talked to the DCI. Natalie led her into a side interview room.

'I'm sorry, Mrs Hartwell, I understand that you have some concerns?'

'Concerns? I'm staggered by your insensitivity!'

Natalie was taken aback.

'My poor fifteen-year-old daughter, a child, has just been raped by three strangers, including at knife point, in her own bedroom in the family home while we were all held hostage, and your staff see fit to interview her without her mother present, and for a male doctor to examine her! How do you think that made her feel? Two men standing over her, albeit one her father, and one wearing surgical gloves, very like the rapists used, ordering her to lay on her back with her legs wide open while he proceeds to invade her again, without, according to my husband, even a word of comfort or reassurance? I'm appalled, simply appalled!'

'I'm so sorry, Mrs Hartwell, it's not meant to be like that, I assure you. As it happens, the officers who dealt with your daughter today aren't the usual staff that deal with such cases and as such would not have been aware to the same extent of the sensitivities. The doctor, however, will have done this many times.'

'That's no comfort to us today, is it? The officer who interviewed her and took a statement, again a man, simply didn't seem to believe her and seemed distracted by the time lapse and the difficulty by now of obtaining forensic evidence from the first rape. My husband said it was more like having someone receive a report of a stolen bicycle than someone dealing with a rape victim! We've suffered enough and don't need to be handled like this by the very people who are charged to protect us!'

As Jan Hartwell left in tears, DCI Natalie Goodwin was left to reflect on how things had gone so far. Handling the main incident she felt had gone well, but clearly the follow-up process had not been handled as she would have liked. She went away feeling disappointed and frustrated but determined to get the appointment of a suitable female liaison officer for the family right. Her immediate thought was to deploy DC Kate Baker. Kate had plenty of experience in this area having supported families through child kidnap cases and sudden bereavement many times. She was kindly, but realistic, too, which most of the people she had dealt with had seemed to appreciate. For now, however, she was conscious that her duty lay with the investigation.

Chaff had been taken to a different hospital to Sam, under guard. During surgery a sharp-eyed nurse had noticed irregularities in his hair line, and the false beard and facial hair had been easily removed whilst he was under anaesthetic and two surgeons worked on his wound. The message was quickly relayed to the police, who wasted no time exposing Charlie and Dog and sending out the changed description to all ports and airports. By this time a certain smartly dressed country gent had arrived in France, handed in his Land Rover to the hire company and was sitting on a train enjoying a sandwich, while thinking of his fortune and his future. Barry had got away.

*

The house was searched for evidence and local people were interviewed to help build up the picture of events. Forensic evidence revealed several fingerprints from when members of the gang had been careless and some clear footprints from Charlie and Dog in the mud along the track to the footbridge.

In interview all three men denied responsibility. Charlie and Dog claimed to have been innocently walking down the track when they were confronted by police officers and arrested, which was an affront to their personal liberty. Both claimed no knowledge of the theft of the paintings, the hostage-taking at the house, or the rape. Even Chaff, who had been arrested naked in the house, claimed to have just arrived, saying he was getting ready for a shower having taken no part in the theft, earlier events in the house or the rape.

DCI Goodwin was coming to realise that perhaps the key challenge for the investigation was to link evidence between the two sites: the pharmaceutical company and the house, to make a rock solid case against the three men in police custody. Of course, none of them would name or implicate Barry, but in time under further questioning when stronger evidence was laid before them they started to crack and blame each other. With the detailed statements from the family and the forensic evidence, DCI Goodwin became more confident that she had a strong enough case to present to the Crown Prosecution Service for their view.

Establishing a case against all three men for aggravated burglary, assault and criminal damage had proved to be relatively straight forward, she thought. The original theft and the rape however were more difficult. The theft had been well conducted from the gang's point of view, leaving no fingerprints. Witness statements did, however, establish a link between the descriptions of the four men involved in both incidents. It was decided not to pursue a charge of animal cruelty in relation to the family dog after finding the animal in the barn together with the crossbow, given all the other matters.

Under pressure, Henry Stewart-Montague had sacrificed the inside man in order to save himself. Pascal had been arrested in Spain and at least that one painting had been recovered. Even with this evidence, however, the case against the gang for the theft of nine paintings was far from watertight.

The lawyers for the three defendants had argued strongly that only six paintings were involved and of course didn't mention the gold bars. Natalie wanted to nail down Henry but had to accept that whilst she was sure he had been involved and the implication was that he had taken one or two paintings himself, she wasn't going to convince the CPS to prosecute, let alone a court to convict him. There was some compensation she supposed though in adding the three extra paintings to the case against the gang for good measure.

Proving rape was, however, much more difficult. Natalie was about to review the evidence with Andy Pickles.

'What have we got then Andy?'

'Well, ma'am, the medical examination revealed the presence of semen, which matches that of the defendant, Chaff. Also the existence of bruising and abrasions consistent with forced sex. So I reckon a rape charge will stand against Chaff, whose real name is Jimmy Godfrey, by the way. He's got form for theft and burglary but nothing sexual. The doctor also reports older bruising consistent with an earlier attack, although obviously with the time lag and several showers in between there is no direct DNA evidence to link Charlie and Dog with the first rape. None of them are admitting rape and are most unlikely to now that they know she was in fact only fifteen, which would make them not only sex offenders, but child sex offenders and thus would ensure a hard time in prison.'

'My heart bleeds!' Natalie replied.

'The witness statements are quite strong though, ma'am. The timing, the observations of the family all identify Charlie and Dog, that is Charlie O'Toole and Danny Hunter as going upstairs with April.'

'And her statement, Andy?'

'It's OK. She obviously found all this really tough, but there's enough there.'

'And how will she stand up as a witness?'

'Um, that's a hard one to call – not the best and not the worst, I suppose. Depends how intrusive the defence barrister is.'

'So, could be difficult. It sounds like we are going to be dependent on the witnesses persuading the jury; it's going to be their word against the gang.'

'I guess so.'

'Any progress yet on tracing Barry or the paintings, Andy?'

'No, ma'am, a complete blank.'

'Any more thoughts on why they targeted the Hartwells?'

'Yes, ma'am, I haven't had a chance to mention it. It seems from snippets from them and from our information that it was the house that was identified in advance, not the Hartwell family themselves. Charlie O'Toole apparently spent some time in the area as a child and remembered this isolated house. Also, ma'am, the time lag we talked about, it appears that the gang went north after swopping vehicles in the lorry park, presumably as a decoy. They were all soaking wet on arrival at the house. It had been raining, so I wonder if they dumped or buried the removal firm's overalls on the way.'

'Yes possibly, not that it's particularly important at this stage, but thanks for the explanation.'

*

By now Barry had crossed Western Europe mostly by train without difficulty. In Berlin he bought all the necessary equipment to reinvent himself again as a biker and set off on a smart touring motorbike to complete his journey into Bulgaria. It was there that he had planned to meet Herman and to receive his share of the proceeds from the sale. He was expecting a good deal. Herman didn't let him down. By the time they had met, Herman had purchased an impressive house in the mountains with some land, and had made arrangements for some repairs and acquisition of household goods, which all helped to dispose of some of the money without attracting too much attention. There was also a 4x4 in the barn and some basic farm equipment. Barry could play the part of an enterprising pioneer to emerging Eastern Europe with little chance of detection, he thought.

The sale had gone well, with all the paintings accounted for and Herman had no difficulty selling gold on legitimate markets. He was able to hand Barry a substantial holdall of cash in different currencies, the paperwork for the house and various investments and bank deposits. Barry was quite overwhelmed by the comprehensive service and didn't even ask what it had cost him. Herman knew from experience that his approach would dazzle and confuse such petty criminals and leave them feeling that they had a good deal. Whilst he knew it was only really the small change, at least one of the paintings had raised far more than they had expected, but that was business after all.

Chapter Seven

A few days after the awful events at the family home, Mark was planning on returning to work and believed that Sam was showing some early signs of recovery having been discharged from hospital. No specific damage had been found but the medical team had been keen to stress that problems could well occur for some time. Jan remained sceptical about Mark's plans and was concerned that his apparent optimism was probably unfounded. She also worried about Sam; he had taken such a beating. April, however, was clearly struggling, and making no attempt to hide it. She was moody, bad tempered and very easily upset. Jan felt it really was like walking on eggshells, particularly for her as the family arbitrator, even more than usual with her teenage daughter.

The family had spent a few days away in a rented cottage not too far from home, both to get away from it and to leave the police alone to do what they had to do in the house. Whilst feelings were understandably very raw in the immediate aftermath, none of them were sure whether they could face returning to live there in the longer term.

Conversations in the house were partly based on hope, but also on anger. Emotions were running high. Mark felt guilty that he had gone out that night at all. He felt terrible that he had failed to protect his daughter and worried that Jan felt that he had left them again when he went for help. None of this helped preserve a marriage that was already faltering. Over the years, Mark and Jan had grown apart and other than the children, now had little in common. At this early stage he felt in his bones that this could drive them apart. In some ways he felt that might be for the best, but equally, at the moment they all really needed to be solid, for each other.

Jan felt angry and desperately sad for April. This was no way to encounter sex or launch into adulthood, and she knew from the start that the impact on April would be long lasting. She didn't think that Mark had handled the whole situation at all well and was disappointed. She wondered how she would deal with that. Would she forgive, or would the feelings linger? Jan was also worried about Sam, who had only just started work as a surveyor with a local firm before the incident. Jobs were hard to come by and she didn't want him to lose this one.

Sam was still feeling the immediate after effects of being battered by two baseball bats. He still felt sick and had headaches and he had started to notice that it had affected his balance, too. He was also worried about his job and how he would manage to concentrate and keep up in his new role. The firm were initially supportive but his dad had warned him that this wouldn't last and that they would expect him to get back to full speed sooner rather than later. In trying to review his options, he wondered whether the firm would allow him a temporary break, a sort of gap year, although he knew that his father would disapprove.

April had spent much of her time just sitting on the sofa subdued, staring into space wanting to hug the cushions and rejecting them at the same time. She was finding difficulty in sleeping and felt most uncomfortable going into her bedroom in the cottage, and whilst she knew that at least three of the men were behind bars, she felt that they would all come back and find her and want to do it all again. She certainly didn't feel like going back to school.

Mark tried to make light of things. 'Come on folks,' he suggested, 'it's a nice day, lets go for a walk. There's a path down to the river and into some woods nearby. Let's explore.'

With some reluctance they did all set off for a walk eventually. It was times like this that they also realised how much they missed their poor dog. He had been all but forgotten in the context of everything else. The thought of possibly having another one hadn't really occurred to anyone as yet; so much had changed.

'So do you feel ready to get back to work, Sam?' asked his dad.

'Not yet, Dad, give it another week. I hope these headaches will stop and I stop feeling dizzy.'

'OK, son, so do I, but you can't wait too long.'

'How about you, April, are you alright?' he asked, as Jan glared at him and gestured 'alright?' behind April.

'I feel like shit, Dad. I'm still in pain and I just can't get it out of my head...' she replied, starting to cry.

'Oh you really are a clot sometimes, Mark! How do you think she feels?' Jan cried.

'Well, sometimes you have to get on with it. That's what my dad said after the war,' Mark replied flatly.

'Dad, I can't just get on with it! This has ruined my life!' cried April sobbing and turning away from him. She started heading back to the cottage.

'Look what you've done now!' shouted Jan in exasperation!

Before he could stop himself Mark blurted out insensitively, 'Bloody hell, she's only been...'

'Don't! Just don't!' Outraged, Jan cut him off firmly and started walking back with her.

'Come on lad, there must be a pub down here,' said Mark carrying on walking. Sam felt torn, but thought he'd better stay with his father on this occasion.

They carried on walking, with Mark trying to convince himself that everything would return to normal in a few days, and Sam trying to explain that he didn't know where this was going to leave him at the moment, let alone thoughts of a return to work. The two conversations continued in parallel with little connection.

They tramped on in silence along the unfamiliar path, both alone in their thoughts, isolated, unconnected, with Sam still feeling ill and confused. Neither knowing how to handle it or express it and Mark trying to find comfort in being oblivious to it. They walked on for some time until Mark saw it first.

'Look ahead son, there you go, The Rose and Crown, freehouse! Come on.'

Reluctantly Sam followed his father into the pub, thinking that this wasn't a good idea and wasn't going to help with the headaches. After a couple of pints he knew that he was right as he headed for the toilet to throw up.

'What's wrong with you, lad? Same again?' his father asked him rhetorically as he ordered another round, determined to try to drown his sorrows.

'Dad, Dad, I really don't feel good.'

'Never mind, just get this down you!' was the unsympathetic response. 'It'll do you good!'

Sam struggled through his beer and tried to persuade his father that they really should head off back as the police family liaison officer was due to visit that afternoon; someone called DC Kate Baker. Mark grumbled all the way back whilst Sam stumbled and was sick several times in the undergrowth.

When they got back to the cottage Kate was already there and Jan wasn't pleased. She guessed that Mark would have taken Sam to a pub and equally that it was a stupid idea. She could see that Sam didn't look at all well. She greeted him sympathetically at the back door and just glared at Mark again, who shook his head in disbelief as they all walked in to meet Kate.

'I've just arrived, Mr Hartwell. I'm pleased to meet you all. I'm Kate Baker and will be your FLO throughout what will no doubt be a very difficult time for you. I'm here to support you.'

'We won't need much of that,' responded Mark, 'we prefer to sort our own problems out. Things will be OK in a week or two.'

'I don't think so dear;' responded Jan, 'anyway the officer's here to help.'

'The role of the FLO is to provide the victims of serious crime a single point of contact with the police 24/7. Then, to help support them, provide information and explain what's happening with the investigation and court process.'

'That's up to you, love. You've got 'em, you jail 'em. It's not our business now,' said Mark with mild hostility.

'I'm sorry, Mr Hartwell, but it's not as simple as that; we are likely to need all of you to give evidence in court if these men are to be convicted,' Kate replied.

'What do you mean? You caught the bastards red-handed; they'll just go to jail, forever as far as I'm concerned!' Mark responded indignantly.

'You are all part of that process, I'm afraid, Mr Hartwell. If it goes to trial, which seems likely at this point, then you will all need to give evidence in open court and a judge will decide if they go to prison or not and for how long. That's the English legal system.'

'We just want to get on with our lives, love, without all this hassle. Who's in control of this process anyway? Sounds like they are being allowed to call the shots!'

'Mark, you may just want to get on with it and imagine it didn't happen, but we don't all feel like that, dear,' said Jan quietly and calmly.

'I don't ever want to see those men again – in court, in prison, anywhere!' said April firmly, as the tears started to roll again.

'I'm really sorry, believe me I am, but you all have to realise just what an impact an event like this will have on your lives. You may like to think its over, but the truth is it's far from over yet, and if you want to see these men get what they deserve you will have to help the legal process to achieve that. I know it's painful, I know it's difficult. I have been through this with lots of individuals and families and people cope with it in different ways. I'm here to help you, if you let me, but I'm not here to impose anything on you.'

After a silence, Kate calmly got up from her chair and left a card with her contact details on for each of them. 'I'm going to leave it there now. Please think about what I've said and please feel free to contact me at any time. Thank you.'

As Kate left she didn't have a good feeling about this case at all.

Returning to the station, Natalie saw her come in and asked, 'How did you get on?'

'Not good, I'm afraid. There was a terrible atmosphere in the house. They may have seemed united initially, but there are serious differences emerging now and I was left with reservations about how much cooperation we might get.'

'What do you mean?'

'Well, the husband and wife clearly don't get on, at least not at the moment, and the offspring look caught in the middle. The husband appears fixed in his thinking and resistant, with no understanding of the realities of the court process, and poor April just looks completely traumatised and scared rigid. I don't anticipate her being any good as a witness at this stage.'

'Oh, I see,' replied the DCI. 'You are going to have your work cut out then. I'm glad I put you on the case, Kate. You're the best we've got. Just keep me informed. I trust your judgement, but I do want to see these guys go down for a very long time.'

'Yes, ma'am, so do I,' replied Kate sombrely.

Back in the house an argument had developed; simmering tensions that were dormant and under the surface were emerging under the pressure of recent events. Jan and Mark were at loggerheads, April was upset and Sam felt confused. They needed help and they needed it fast – if only they could recognise it.

Meanwhile, back in the police custody suite, questioning the prisoners continued before the prospect of the first hearing in court. The three men had been kept apart and had largely stuck to their stories of innocence or minimum involvement. None of them had admitted rape or any sexual element to the case at all. Encouraged by their lawyers, they all felt confident to sit back and challenge the court to prove it, knowing that medical evidence would be limited and the lead witness was likely to be flaky. Having said that, outline discussions had already indicated that if they were convicted for aggravated burglary, in these circumstances they could easily be looking at ten years imprisonment. That would be without even considering the impact of the paintings. They knew the evidence against them for the theft wasn't as strong as the aggravated burglary. They knew the system and would play the game. They had arranged alibis for the theft, which they hoped would stand up, with mates prepared to testify in court that the four men were all with them at the time the crime was committed. It hadn't been so easy to anticipate what might happen in the house however, so nothing had been put in place. The best they could hope for was to get away with the rapes and reduce the aggravated burglary to straight burglary and assault. In that case, without the paintings or the rapes, with their records they reckoned on about three years at best, which meant they'd be out in eighteen months, with about six months of that served in cushy conditions on remand and could then retire and move abroad with the money from the paintings and the gold. Not a bad deal, they reckoned, if they could get it!

*

On the day of the first hearing Kate was attempting to support the family and keep them informed. The CPS had scrutinised the papers and were aiming in the first instance at a remand in custody, just to secure the men and reassure the family while the legal process ran its course.

They judged that this was not likely to be contentious because there clearly was a risk to the family as key witnesses, and a risk of absconding if they were given bail. Realistically on such serious charges they felt that bail wasn't an option.

The CPS had considered charging the three men with attempted murder for the assault on Sam, but felt that it wouldn't stick, so pitched in with malicious wounding with intent and aggravated burglary in the first instance. They succeeded in persuading the court to order a remand in custody pending further investigations while the crown prepared its case for the theft and rape charges.

While being driven away from court in separate prison vans to separate remand prisons around the London area, all three men were feeling uneasy that it might not go to plan as well as they thought; three years now looked optimistic, it may be as much as ten.

Kate explained the court process to the family and reassured them that realistically she couldn't see the men being released from custody until either sentence or trial, which meant that they were safe.

April felt the most relieved; this was real reassurance for her at least. Mark was trying to adapt to their new circumstances but was still resistant and not comfortable with this level of intrusion. As the family asked more questions it felt like snakes and ladders, with progress being constantly followed by a fall.

'So Kate, on these charges, is that it now? How long will they get?' asked Jan.

'Oh, we are a long way from that yet,' Kate replied. 'If these charges alone stick, they could be looking at around ten years.'

'Thank God for that!' replied Jan. 'So at least ten years knowing they'll be inside and we'll be safe!'

'Well, no, Jan. It doesn't work like that. A ten year sentence means five years in custody and five on licence, supervised by the probation service.'

'What! Why doesn't ten mean ten? Probation? You mean do-gooders letting these monsters do as they like?' challenged Jan.

'Yes, don't probation look after young people in trouble?' added Mark.

'I'm sorry, there is often all kinds of confusion in the public's understanding of all this, until or unless like you, you have to face it head on. The law is the same for everybody and it has to take into account competing interests and factors; protecting the public, giving the victim some sense of justice and at the same time trying to rehabilitate, or to turn round the offender.

'Probation these days is a very different animal to what people often believe. I know many probation officers and have the greatest respect for most of them. They oversee or supervise the most difficult, dangerous and damaged offenders in the community and they do it well, for the most part. These days, we all work together much better so the police and other agencies will all contribute to planning for these men's eventual release and monitoring. But more of that later; come on, let's have a cup of tea,' said Kate, trying to break the tension.

The family sat together with Kate round the table in the kitchen, trying to take in all this information.

'So Kate, as the victims in this, we will be protected, won't we?' asked Jan.

'Jan, I will do all I can to ensure you are safe and that you are kept informed, yes.'

'That's not quite the same thing, is it?' replied Mark.

Kate smiled, but couldn't give them the copper bottomed guarantee that they seemed to be searching for or expecting. This job was hard, she thought. Then she remembered some good news. She remembered her recent conversation with the CPS.

'Oh, I do have some good news. The CPS have looked at April's actions in the incident and decided not to press any charges for wounding or assault in relation to stabbing Chaff,' she announced, hoping for a positive reaction.

Jan looked bemused, April looked insulted and Mark ready to explode and throw her out of the house.

'What is this!' cried Mark, standing up and waving his arms about.

'Do you seriously expect us to believe that after being held captive in our own house, assaulted and April raped, that when in order to escape the ordeal she struck her abuser with the very knife that he had threatened her with, that the legitimate authorities would even consider for a moment that April could possibly be blamed for anything?' spluttered Jan.

'Let alone prosecuted! What is this? Those bastards are the ones to be blamed! Not us!' shouted Mark.

Kate had obviously misjudged the moment and unintentionally enflamed an already raw and tense situation. She felt it was better that she left. She made her apologies as best she could and left the family in pieces, feeling victimised and abused again.

Chapter Eight

April was due to return to see her GP, Doctor Dita Bajek. She was from Poland and was a very calm and kindly young woman. As she entered the surgery with her mum, April felt very anxious.

'They are not going to examine me again, are they, Mum?' she asked.

'I don't know, love. You'll have to wait and see, but I'll be with you.'

After a short wait they were called through.

'Good morning April; Mrs Hartwell,' said Dr Bajek as she welcomed them in. 'Firstly I have to say how sorry I am to have heard about your ordeal. It must have been terrible.'

'Yes, it was,' replied Jan as April nodded.

The doctor sensitively asked some basic questions and began to get an outline picture of some level of recovery, physically at least.

'Right, I will need to examine you,' she said, as she got up and put on her surgical gloves.

April fainted.

The doctor was surprised but reacted calmly and with empathy, making April comfortable on the couch, whilst reassuring her as she came round that she had no intention of hurting her or doing anything against her will, but that it was in her best interests that she check things were alright 'down below'. Whilst April composed herself the doctor discreetly explained to her mother that there was obviously some risk of infection, which if present needed to be treated as early as possible.

The examination proceeded and the doctor was satisfied that April was healing, but took some blood to test for infection, just in case. She asked further questions and advised on warning signs if any infection was to develop.

'April, after such a traumatic incident, recovery is often prolonged and difficult. The body will heal fairly quickly, but the mind can take much longer. I don't want to put you under any pressure but I would encourage you to consider counselling to help deal with some of the feelings that I'm sure you will be experiencing. How are you sleeping by the way?'

'Not well. I wake up sweating, dreaming, worrying; it's horrible!' said April, managing to reply without tears.

After further discussion April and her mother took the doctor's advice and left the surgery leaving treatment options open. They all felt that April needed time to consider what Dr Bajek had said and that whilst counselling may be beneficial, she was not ready for that yet. At least they felt some reassurance that the immediate physical effects were healing.

As a young doctor, Dr Bajek had not had to deal with such an extreme case as this in her short career so far and felt quite affected by the experience. She so wanted to help and support April and sincerely hoped that she would be able to. As well as direct feelings for April in this situation, the circumstances also reminded her of stories from home of Polish history and abuse following invasion from both Germany and Russia; of memories of the news of the Bosnian crisis and of some experiences of her own and of her friends whilst studying medicine.

There is nothing new in sexual exploitation, she thought, it's just sad that it continues.

Other members of the family were also grappling with their own adjustments. Mark returned to work and welcomed some relative normality. His mates didn't know what to say, so they opted to say very little after an initial courteous 'Sorry to hear about...' Mark wasn't unhappy about this response and just wanted to forget the whole affair and get on with things.

Sam felt some improvement and his GP suggested that to try to get back to normal and return to work was probably sensible, but he did warn him that the symptoms he was suffering from could well persist, though hopefully would diminish over time. Sam tried to explain this to his boss but got the impression that he thought as a young man Sam should just get over it. In a way he was glad to be back at work, similar to his dad, but remained concerned about where all this would leave him in the longer term.

*

April and her mum set off to visit her school and were reassured that Kate as part of her role came with them. They saw the head, who didn't really seem to have much insight into April's situation, and like Sam's employer and to some extent her dad, seemed to expect her to brush it off and concentrate on her GCSEs. They tried to negotiate some guided work at home and a return in stages.

April said she didn't know what she would say to her mates. The head had to inform her that as the incident had been both on the TV news and in the press, nationally initially and had continued to be covered locally, there was little doubt that her mates would know. He added that he would ask teachers to keep an eye on it and to mention to their classes to be sensitive.

April felt that she may struggle with male teachers and felt very anxious about PE with the prospect of nudity and showers. The head told her not to be embarrassed and that Miss Fairbright, the head of PE, would look after her. April smiled as she remembered that the whole school was sure that Miss Fairbright was gay and that she made some of the girls feel uncomfortable in the changing room already!

*

Over the next few months things did settle down somewhat, although Christmas was grim. No one felt like celebrating, wearing silly hats or playing Monopoly. They couldn't raise the enthusiasm to cook a turkey and had eaten frozen pizza. After the New Year the boys were back at work. April did return to school and Jan continued as the family mum and coordinator, operating from their temporary home in the rented house. She kept in touch with Kate, who just told her that the investigation was continuing OK, and that she would give her plenty of warning before any potential trial dates.

Jan and Mark continued to drift apart. In fact he was working away in another office more and more and started renting a room there. Eventually he got a flat and only returned home at weekends.

After the police had finished their search of the house, the family were free to return, but all had reservations. April certainly felt that she could never sleep in that room again. After several days of visits back and forth they all agreed that it just didn't feel the same and that they felt that they couldn't return.

They continued to rent the cottage in the meantime and Kate had advised them not to make any longer term plans too soon. This arrangement was, however, stretching the family finances, and out of necessity they decided to rent out the family house for twelve months initially.

The search continued for Barry, and the three prisoners just bided their time, protested their innocence and looked forward to a trial.

The family were almost starting to feel like they could relax a bit more and were trying not to focus on what was to come. None of them looked forward to the prospect of having to be in court.

Chapter Nine

Mark was in his office when his phone registered receipt of a text message. He carried on until it was convenient to look at it. When he did he went cold. Mark left his desk on the pretext of getting something, went downstairs, and sat outside in his car. He opened the text message, put on his glasses and breathed deeply. The message read:

Your case will come to trial. You & your family will not cooperate with the police or give evidence. You have been warned.

Mark sat still for a moment to get his breath. What now? Should I just delete it? Should I obey it? Should I tell Kate; tell Jan? What to do? He weighed it up for a moment and decided. Bollocks, Jan thinks I let her down over the incident, I'm not going to risk doing that again if I have any chance of saving my marriage, he thought. He knew he had wanted to just move on and forget it – Jan was right in that respect, but now in a sense this made it different. He certainly didn't want to be bullied into walking away. No, now it was more that he wanted to get even. He decided to ring Kate.

In the police incident room DCI Goodwin was assessing and reviewing the evidence so far. Another report came in of a potential sighting of Barry. He'd already been seen all over the country and in at least ten places abroad! Her scepticism again proved to be accurate – when they checked out the report it was an innocent man with no connections to the case, and incidentally, a pretty poor look alike anyway. She reflected on how much police time got wasted chasing dead ends from members of the public genuinely wanting to help but actually hindering the investigation.

A phone rang again and this time it was Kate's phone. She had just joined the team for the review meeting.

'Kate, it's Mark Hartwell. I'm out of my depth here, Kate. I've had a threatening text message. I think you ought to see it.'

'OK, what does it say?' she asked. Mark read her the message and she agreed to meet him.

'Something?' asked Natalie.

'Yes, it's Mark Hartwell. He's had a threatening text message. I'm just going to see him now.'

'How are the family coping?'

'They are struggling.'

'OK, keep me informed.'

Kate found Mark still sitting in his car waiting in the car park at work. She pulled up and got in beside him. He looked shocked.

'Hi Kate; thanks for coming. Hey, I know I've given you something of a hard time, I'm sorry. I don't mean anything by it, I'm just struggling with all of this, you know?' said Mark trying to build bridges.

'It's OK, Mark, I don't take offence. I've got a skin like a rhino!' she replied, and they laughed. 'So what about this message; have you told anyone else yet?'

'No, Kate, just you.'

'OK,' she replied feeling privileged.

'So, what do you think? Some kind of nutter or is it more serious?' Mark asked.

'It's serious, Mark. This is no nutter, this is someone who knows – my guess is, put up to it by the gang. Sadly, it's not unusual and we have all sorts of measures to protect witnesses, so you mustn't worry. You're not going to buckle are you?'

Mark explained about his thinking, about him and Jan and he had to acknowledge that it felt good to talk. Kate appreciated his honesty and that he had felt able and willing to disclose this to her and to her alone at this stage.

'Mark, I'll tell what I'll do. I'll take your phone away, if I may, and make some enquires. The tech boys will probably to able to trace it and if so we'll go round and read the riot act to however sent it.'

'Do these sorts of threats happen a lot then?'

'I'm afraid so and it's a growing trend, fed by technology. But don't worry, I feel confident we can handle it.'

'This is another world Kate, isn't it? And not one I'm used to. Most of the public never see this side of life,' Mark said thoughtfully.

'You are right, Mark, spot on,' responded Kate.

*

Sam was having a bad day at work. He felt he couldn't concentrate and was struggling with the headaches. He hoped that it would pass. It did improve slightly over the next few weeks, but was still troublesome.

April remained subdued and moody. The tests concluded that she had developed an infection, almost certainly related to the rape, and with all the emotion and sleep disturbance it knocked her for six. She really felt quite ill. Doctor Bajek was very understanding. She still hoped that April would seek counselling, but accepted that it would not be now.

Kate did some investigation relating to Mark's phone and found a link to Charlie in prison. It appeared that he had used a contact outside to attempt to influence Mark. Charlie was given a stern reminder that he was yet to be in court, and prison security committed to monitor all future calls. The police also logged the information carefully, as intimidating witnesses would be a factor for the judge to consider in sentencing if they were eventually convicted. The person who sent the message was visited by the local police and warned off. The same officers were delighted to oblige later that same evening when they stopped him driving his car erratically and were able to arrest him for drink driving. When it came to court later, with his record he was sentenced to eighteen months in custody which would take him well clear of the trial.

Over the next couple of months April was mostly unwell. One infection followed another and then colds and viruses all struck in turn. She was starting to feel run down and was losing weight. She felt tired all the time. Jan was worried about her, especially as she was very moody and withdrawn. Dr Bajek was keeping a close eye on her progress and had ordered a variety of further tests.

April was ready for the doctor's appointment to hear the results, hoping her infection had gone. 'Come on, Mum, let's go. I want to hear that at last I'm all clear; I've had enough antibiotics!'

They arrived at the surgery to see the duty doctor, who had just joined the practice and didn't know the case. As they walked in he looked relaxed, and April was relieved.

'Yes,' he said, 'all your blood tests are clear now.'

'Oh, that's such a relief!' said Jan, smiling at April.

As they got up to go, the doctor just looked up and said casually, 'Oh, I don't know whether congratulations are in order, but I assume you realise that you are three months pregnant?'

Chapter Ten

The CPS reported their satisfaction with the quality of the case. They felt able to present it to court optimistic of three convictions with substantial sentences. They anticipated that given the seriousness of the rape by three strangers – if the jury believed April – her illness aggravated by sexually transmitted infection, her pregnancy, her age and threats with a weapon, that the judge would consider a life sentence for that alone. If the case was proved on all counts – including the art theft – against all three men, it was clear that they would not be released for a very long time. However, all this was speculation at this stage and had to be tested in court.

Natalie and her team were still busy trying to tie up any loose ends and check the evidence again and again. They knew that they would be heavily dependent on April's testimony in court, particularly if the rape charge was to stick against Charlie and Dog for the first assault. Kate was still working on preparing April for the ordeal and they hadn't yet decided whether to use a screen to protect her or to expose her to open court and the glare of the defendants and their families.

There was still nothing solid on Barry, although unlikely sightings had been reported in France, and also by expats in South America and South Africa. The investigation against him was effectively dormant. None of the money had been secured, with only one of the paintings discovered so far. Art specialists in the police were happy to play the long game however. Henry's evidence from the inventory, though suspect, did identify specifics about each painting, and at some stage they would appear on international markets for sale and then the authorities could pounce.

A court date was imminent. The three defendants were to meet their respective solicitors in prison before what would usually be only a short interview with their barristers in the cells at Crown Court on the day.

When the solicitors did visit, there were some differences in the position for each of the three men. The witness statements indicated that only two of the three defendants had assaulted Sam. Subsequently they had all blamed each other. The outcome of that could prove to be crucial. There was also some scope for legal argument about the definition of aggravated burglary, which the crown had based on threats and violence, which was beyond dispute, but the element of theft was based on theft of the family's mobile phones and this was disputed as the phones hadn't actually left the property. They had, however, all been smashed, with arguably the intent to permanently deprive. Charlie and dog were advised that their story about just walking down the track when they were caught wouldn't stand up, nor would Chaff's story that he had only just entered the house when he was arrested. Their alibis for the original theft, however, were quite credible; total fabrication, but nevertheless quite credible. It would be the rape evidence that would make the critical difference. Chaff was advised that he would be convicted, but the others hoped that they could cast enough doubt after the first rape to leave the jury unconvinced. Charlie felt 'well aggrieved' that his mate outside had let him down and was unable to 'persuade' the family not to testify. He'd now left him seriously in the shit, he thought.

*

By now April was sixteen and was gutted by the news of her pregnancy. At age fifteen, at the time of the incident, she had only kissed a few boys at school. She knew the basic biology and knew that her attackers hadn't used a condom, but all the talk had been about infection, no one had mentioned pregnancy. This seemed so unfair. Another blow! Together she and Jan sat in the surgery in floods of tears. Different staff walked by and offered their help but this wasn't going to be a quick or easy fix – difficult decisions would have to be made.

One of the nurses who knew the family and had worked closely with Dr Bajek took them aside into a private room.

'I appreciate how difficult this must be for you, but now is probably not the best time to decide what next. Give yourself some time, dear.'

'How can they just do that and walk away!' shouted April. 'I don't want a child – I'm barely sixteen myself! And I certainly don't want their child!' she sobbed as she stood up to be sick. All the benefit and relief from the blood test results had now ebbed away and she felt instantly ill again, completely exhausted and now faced yet another mountain to climb.

The nurse made April an appointment to see Dr Bajek, and mother and daughter left distraught, arm in arm.

Driving home, Jan wondered what they had done to deserve all this. This was about as much as she could take. She hadn't really thought about the possibility of pregnancy and had assumed that the medics would have thought of that at the time. What would Mark say? She thought he would want to go to the three prisons and tear them down brick by brick until he could find the three men and pull them limb from limb.

April returned to staring into empty space. Again she felt numb. This just wasn't fair!

When they got home, Jan braced herself but thought she must ring Mark, just as the phone began to ring. Maybe that's him now, she thought, wanting to hear the results. She answered the phone only to hear the school secretary asking in a sanctimonious manner why April wasn't in school, again.

Mark was gutted by the news, too, and despite Jan's fears did not threaten to chase off straight away to attack the prisons, but was calm and tried his best to be supportive. He promised to finish early and get home as soon as he could. When he came off the phone one of the others walked into his office and made some crass joke, but instantly wished that he hadn't.

'Oh dear, whatever it is mate, you go to your family and do what you need to do. I'll sort out here, honestly, just go.'

Mark felt broken, got up from his desk without even collecting his pen or his diary and walked out.

That evening the family sat in the rented cottage feeling again that their lives were in tatters. They decided not to disturb Sam, but to leave him at work. Jan made some tea and tried to make light conversation, but the obvious was looming over them.

'I don't want it. I'm not having it. I want an abortion,' April said quietly.

'Well, there are other options, love. I don't think, as the nurse said, that we need to rush,' responded Jan trying desperately to be diplomatic.

'No, Mum, you're not listening. I said I'm going to have an abortion.'

'She is only sixteen, Jan, but on this occasion, I do think this is April's decision and that we should support her in whatever she decides,' said Mark sombrely.

'Thanks, Dad,' replied April, with a rare daughter to dad smile.

After the tea had gone cold, April went up to her bedroom to cry and Jan started feverously cleaning to occupy the void, while Mark announced that he was going to the pub.

Dr Bajek rang as soon as she heard the news and offered to come round and see April at home later. By the time April had stopped crying, there was nothing left to clean. Mark had woken up in the chair after returning home drunk, when Dr Bajek arrived. She looked drawn.

'I'm so sorry,' she said to Jan. I didn't want to worry her about the risk of pregnancy, so I suppose I put it out of my mind. Also, a morning after pill would have been too late after the first time, so I suppose it wasn't considered when April was first treated. She's so young, but obviously biologically her body is ready to produce a child. How is she feeling?'

'How do you think?' replied Jan holding back the tears. She's been upstairs crying most of the time since we got home. Dr Bajek, she seems set on having an abortion.'

'Well, we can consider the options, but I must admit, I think that's how I'd feel, wouldn't you, carrying a child conceived by rape?'

'I suppose so,' said Jan sadly. 'I've never had to think about it, but as her mother that's got to be the best approach, hasn't it? I just hope it doesn't affect her chances of having children in the future. Will it, Dr Bajek?'

As she tried to provide reassurance, April heard voices and came downstairs. When she saw the doctor she started to cry again. After a brief discussion, Dr Bajek left her with a prescription to alleviate the viral infection should it return, and something to help her sleep. She promised to make the referral to the consultant at the clinic they used. April seemed relieved.

Chapter Eleven

Members of both sides of the family had tried to offer help, but Mark's only sister lived in Australia and Jan's two brothers hardly spoke to each other and contacted her rarely, so family support, whilst well meaning, in reality was only available on a superficial level. Friends seemed to find it all too difficult and didn't know what to say. Some would even cross the street to avoid an awkward moment. The few neighbours there were decided it was best to leave the family in peace, so apart from their individual contacts the Hartwell family felt pretty much isolated and left to face the situation alone.

Mark did find work a helpful distraction, but Sam was struggling to overcome the effects of the assault. Sometimes he would think he was OK, then it would all come back again, that is the headaches, the dizziness and the lack of concentration. Some of April's girlfriends still visited to try to offer help, but for Jan virtually her sole concentration was on others, with no time to think of her own needs.

Kate and the doctor were probably the best sources of support they had. Kate tried to stay professional, but the role demanded more and she found it hard to cut off. She felt so desperately sorry for the plight the family found themselves in. It was no silver lining but Mark and Jan did seem to her to have managed to grow closer together after at first looking like this would drive them apart. For different reasons, however, it was Sam and April who worried her the most. She particularly worried about how April would stand up to the rigours of the trial and feared that she wouldn't. Kate took every opportunity to coach her along when she could, telling her carefully the format of a trial and roles of the officials, the legal process and so on, but didn't feel like it was really registering with her. April was still feeling quite ill as the viral infection had returned after the shocking news of the pregnancy.

Privately, Dr Bajek had warned Jan that unless April's condition improved it was unlikely that she would be fit enough to withstand an abortion, or could run out of time and may have to go full term and give birth. Jan was horrified at the thought and didn't want to burden April with this possibility. Instead she did her level best to aid her recovery in the hope of avoiding the possibility.

A week later Kate came to visit the family. She thought that April's condition appeared to have improved since her last call. She brought news that despite their best efforts to avoid a trial, the three defendants still all persisted in pleading not guilty and a trial date had been set for three weeks hence. It would start at 10 o'clock on Monday with opening legal arguments and was forecast to last some five or six weeks. Kate could see the disbelief and strain written on their faces. Why was this process so painful, they all thought, this is victimisation for the second or third time. From a layman's point of view, let alone as a victim, they simply couldn't get their heads around the fact that they knew what had happened, had reported it honestly, but felt that they were not believed and hence had to endure a trial. Kate tried hard to explain that it was not like that, but to the Hartwell family that was exactly how it felt.

As those three weeks unfolded and the anticipation and anxiety mounted, tensions in the house were high. April could fly into a temper or display tantrums or tears in an instant. In fairness to Mark he was trying so hard to be tolerant, but was struggling. Sam spent most of his time out of the house to avoid the atmosphere.

A week before the trial, the medics were still debating the feasibility of April's abortion as she started to show signs of pregnancy. This felt like further insult to injury with another assault on her body.

Mark was off work today and Sam had called home on his way to a business call. He said that he was OK, but didn't feel very good. Mark suggested another attempt at the family walk down by the river as spring was in the air, and this time both April and Jan felt like joining him. Sam opted to stay and said he'd carry on to his next call and see them after work.

The three of them set off in the warm spring air with a sense of renewal and hope. The path was now dry and much easier to walk on, particularly for April. They set off down to the river and along the bank. Conversation was light and quite cheerful.

'What do you see us doing after the trial, dear?' asked Jan.

'Oh, I suppose retirement is the next step. Do you think we should sell the house now as none of us seem to have any enthusiasm for returning to live there?' Mark replied.

'I don't want to ever walk through that door again, Dad, honestly,' stated April clearly and firmly.

They passed some other people who noticed April's condition and offered their congratulations.

'Be careful now dear on this path, you don't want to spoil the happy event!' they said.

April tried not to react but just kept on walking while her mother smiled politely. How do I say to people, oh it's not mine, I've been raped actually and am waiting for an abortion, thought April to herself.

When they reached the pub they were in much better spirits than the last time they had gone for a walk together and sat outside while Mark fetched some drinks. April didn't want to go inside and risk a round of glib remarks about taking it easy. She felt she needed a drink, but decided to be pragmatic and have a glass of lemonade. It wasn't its fault after all.

By the time they had ambled back all three of them were feeling far more relaxed and looking forward to a quiet evening at home. Some sense of near normality felt almost comforting.

When they arrived, Jan went straight into the kitchen to make some tea and Mark went into the garage to look for some tools to do a bit of gardening. April walked through into the lounge and was surprised to see Sam still there. He looked to be asleep in the chair. She went over to wake him up as he had obviously forgotten his next call. It was then that April recognised that something wasn't right. Sam looked cold and didn't seem to be breathing. In panic she ran out into the garden shouting, 'Dad, Dad, its Sam, I think he's stopped breathing!' She desperately looked around before she saw her dad cutting some of the hedges in the far corner of the garden.

'Dad, Dad, come quickly, it's Sam; he's in trouble!'

'What April? Has he lost his mobile phone?' Mark retorted in a jovial mood, but soon saw by the look on April's face that she at least thought that this was serious. Mark dropped the shears and ran inside with April to find Sam.

'Dad, what can we do?' screamed April as Jan came into the room, hearing the commotion.

'Ambulance please,' said Mark as the 999 operator answered. 'It's my son, he appears to be unconscious.'

None of the family had any particular expertise in first aid, but Mark did try to establish if he could find a pulse or hear any breathing. It wasn't looking good as they heard the ambulance approaching. Jan froze and it was April who went to open the door to let them in.

Seeing her condition, the ambulance man said, 'Oh dear, is it your husband, madam?'

'No, it's my brother,' she replied to his obvious puzzlement.

The crew started resuscitation and quickly got Sam onto a stretcher and into the back of the ambulance. Jan thought she couldn't face this again as Mark volunteered to join him.

Mark felt that he already knew the outcome, but that there was always hope as they raced through the villages to the hospital.

In A&E a full team worked on Sam for a good twenty minutes before the lead doctor looked up to Mark and had to tell him that unfortunately his son had gone. Sam was pronounced dead.

Initial indications weren't clear but a heart attack or a stroke seemed the most likely cause of death. A post mortem would be required for confirmation. Mark held his son's hand for the last time and kissed him before walking out of the hospital and into the grounds to face a new chapter of horror. Would this nightmare ever end? he wondered as he found a bench to sit on. The person sharing it immediately started to engage him in conversation, something about the cost of parking. Mark wasn't listening as the stranger wittered on.

'Well, my neighbour has to visit her husband you know most days, except on a Wednesday of course and it costs her over £5 a time. People can't afford it you know! Isn't that terrible? Are you visiting today?' he enquired.

'No. I've just lost my only son,' Mark replied quietly, as he took his mobile phone out of his pocket and dialled. 'Jan, it's me,' he said as she answered the phone.

'Yes?'

'It's bad news, love. I'm afraid he's gone. They think he had a heart attack or a stroke.'

Jan turned to April with tears in her eyes – and April knew before her mum relayed the news. Now they had lost a son and a brother. What next? she thought. What possibly could happen next?

Chapter Twelve

It wasn't long before the answer unfolded.

April was sweating and feeling uncomfortable. She started breathing heavily and was in some pain.

'Are you alright, dear?' enquired her mother.

'No. I feel funny... Mum my stomach...it seems to be moving!'

The shock of Sam's death seemed to have induced early labour and after all the debate about the risks, pros and cons of abortion and whether April was strong enough, nature took its course and April was admitted to hospital where she had a miscarriage. Despite the sudden speed of her admission, the staff at the maternity unit seemed well prepared. They were aware of April's circumstances. They dealt with her sensitively in a private room. There were no crass or inappropriate comments on this occasion, only professionalism.

April made no enquiries about the results of her labour; she didn't want to know, and the staff didn't tell. She was cleaned up while someone held her hand, talked gently to her and left her to sleep.

In the circumstances neither Jan nor Mark had felt strong enough to join her in the ambulance straight after losing Sam and April seemed to understand, and in a way felt that this was something she needed to deal with herself. When she woke, both her mum and dad were by her bedside.

April felt relieved; she almost felt cleansed. For her this was to prove to be an important watershed. In a sense, now the rape was over; in a sense, she could now look forward and recovery could begin. There was still a long way to go and it would be a long journey, but April did feel some sense of relief that she could begin to move forward. She started to feel an inner strength that she didn't know she had.

*

News filtered through to Kate about Sam's death, but it wasn't until she rang Jan later that she heard of April's miscarriage. She promised to visit the family when they felt ready and tried to reassure Jan that the trial date would be delayed to allow them some time. She didn't feel it was appropriate to share with her at that stage that these events would trigger a further round of legal argument.

Kate was immediately in touch with the hospital. She explained her position and that she would need to know the paternity of the foetus. The midwife was able to say that the foetus was delivered stillborn and had a mixed race appearance. Therefore in advance of any DNA testing, paternity seemed clearly to relate to Chaff. Kate knew that this would be important in the trial to establish who had been the father. This would settle any argument about whether sex had taken place. Then it was just a matter of consent, and with a fifteen-year-old victim, however callous the defence were, she felt confident that a rape conviction would be secured against Chaff. That meant, however, that the case against the other two for the first assault was growing relatively weaker.

Kate also knew that the post mortem report on Sam would be crucial. She had rung Natalie earlier and was about to review the developments with her.

'That poor family!' said Kate with feeling, as she walked into Natalie's office.

'Yes. What a terrible combination of events!' responded Natalie sympathetically. 'How does anybody deal with that?' she said rhetorically. 'So you said on the phone that you feel confident about securing a rape conviction against Chaff, but a little shaky about the other two men?'

'Yes, that's right. When we have the post mortem report on Sam that could also change the situation dramatically; I'm just wondering what impact the assault had on the cause of death?'

'What do you mean?' replied Natalie, suddenly becoming more interested in the conversation and drawing her mind away from the long list of other cases she was dealing with.

'Well, if the medical view is that the cause of death is either directly attributable to the assault or closely related to it, then we are looking at potential murder or manslaughter convictions. If that happens, whichever combination of them hit Sam with the baseball bats – and the witness evidence suggests Charlie and Dog – they could face life, without even considering the other offences. Natalie, we really could see all of these bastards going away for a very, very long time!'

'Yes, of course. Well done! Keep me informed.'

*

Two weeks later the report arrived on Sam's post mortem. It found the cause of death to be a blood clot on the brain. It suggested that on the balance of probabilities this was probably a delayed reaction to the blows from the baseball bats. In other words, Charlie and Dog had effectively killed him. Natalie was in no doubt that the defence would argue otherwise and produce some medical opinion to support that view, but this was a major breakthrough. She wasted no time in reporting the matter to the CPS for their consideration.

Kate made an appointment to see the family to explain the implications to them. The whole investigation team were very excited.

By contrast, the three gang members waiting in custody were not impressed to hear of the delay and were even less impressed when their respective lawyers visited them in prison and informed them that they may well face a murder charge and a life sentence.

Of course they denied it, but privately Charlie had thought to himself that maybe, just maybe they had gone a little over the top with the kid and the baseball bats, not that in any way he meant to kill him, or for that matter had expected him to die!

Dog was raving mad. He wanted Barry to have his share of the stick – after all, it was all his idea. He was the brains. No one was meant to get hurt, let alone killed – they hadn't taken guns with them after all!

Chaff had exploded back on the wing, punched an officer and sworn at a governor. He was cooling off in the segregation unit. In for a penny, he thought. I'm definitely fucked now!

*

Jan and Mark were sitting in the cottage waiting for Kate, pleased that they had just received an offer on the family house, when the phone rang.

Mark answered; it was the school.

'Hello. Is that April Hartwell's father?' enquired the caller.

'Yes, Mark Hartwell here.'

'Mr Hartwell, I'm Mr Jenkins, head of year. I'm ringing to express my concern about your daughter's school attendance. It really isn't satisfactory. I'm ringing to seek your support to formulate an improvement plan. Mr Hartwell, I must impress on you the importance of your daughter's attendance. It's the reputation of the school at stake. You must realise that we have strict government targets to meet, which if missed would have serious implications for the school.'

'You're not concerned about her education then?' replied Mark dryly.

'Yes, yes, of course, there is that too, but the interests of the school...'

'You know what, Mr Jenkins,' said Mark interrupting 'I don't give a damn about your targets, or the government – any government! After what my daughter's been through this last few months, I'm sure neither does she, and frankly neither should you! Her GCSEs have been disrupted now and we are all due to be in court for several weeks shortly, probably during exam time. What do you want me to do? Tell the judge that April can't be in the witness box because she's got double PE?' said Mark feeling little sympathy for such small-minded trivia.

'Um, um,' replied Mr Jenkins, spluttering, 'no, well perhaps I ought to speak to the head and ask for some home tuition.'

'Yes, you do that. Goodbye,' said Mark, putting the phone down. 'Fucking prat!'

Even Jan laughed. Strangely, their experience did make them realise what was important in life, and Mark had become even less tolerant of what was not!

Kate arrived and they told her the story and she laughed, too. When she told them her news about the case they really didn't know whether to laugh or cry; whether to be pleased or just sad; it all seemed unreal – as if it wasn't really happening to them. Several months ago they had been going about their daily humdrum lives, when a car had pulled onto their drive, and since then their family dog had been killed, their son had been assaulted and had subsequently died, their daughter raped and their family home ruined. Their lives had been turned upside down, and now someone was worried about the school register, while three men they never wanted to see again were rightfully facing potential life imprisonment. It was indeed a strange world!

The following day, Mr Keith, April's English teacher, rang and apologised for his insensitive colleague and offered to see April for home tuition in his own time. He said she was good at English and he didn't want her to miss the chance of a good pass, so would enter her in the exam regardless. April was pleased and felt she could cope with that, but in her mind had let the rest of her GCSEs go. They weren't an immediate priority. This is now. They are for another day, she thought.

PART TWO

THE TRIAL

Chapter Thirteen

Jan, Mark and April gathered together for breakfast on the first morning of the trial. They were due in court at nine o'clock to meet their legal team and had been warned that the first day would largely be about setting the legal context, and not principally about them.

It felt strangely like they were characters in a play waiting for the opening night of a production. There had been plenty of preparation, some publicity and some rehearsals, but now it was time to perform, live.

Despite the concerns and reservations about how well April would stand up to the intensity and rigour of cross examination, she felt strangely empowered and almost confident. She felt that she had recovered from the initial trauma of the miscarriage, at least physically, or had it really actually been an abortion? she pondered. She had made some progress in talking more openly about the mixed bag of emotions involved and was beginning to feel better in some ways. The worst of the infections seemed to have passed and she was gaining strength. Jan and Mark just hoped that it would be enough as they exchanged glances across the table knowing that they shared an anxious sense of trepidation. This was unknown territory for all of them and a whole new area of activity that they had been thrown into; not one that they had chosen, and that in itself was an uncomfortable feeling.

Kate too knew that this was going to be a big day. The trial could easily run to six weeks or more, so she was conscious of the need to help the family pace themselves. Natalie had arranged to be kept closely informed, but of course other work with other cases had to carry on too and take priority, for her at least.

After a quiet, sombre and unenthusiastic breakfast, the family left for court. There was more media interest outside than they had expected. They were quickly ushered into court and to the witness area where they saw their solicitor moving around the corridors. Kate was offering reassurance and trying to keep them calm, whilst April was surprised by the size and scale of the court house. She had expected something smaller and more intimate. It felt quite intimidating. The professionals were all rushing about, seemingly with purpose, but April felt a little lost as she observed and waited.

The three prisoners were in the cells and when produced in court would see each other again for the first time since being arrested. None of them had implicated Barry, although they were all tempted – the criminal code of silence backed with fear of retribution had ensured that. They had, however, over the time of the investigation contradicted themselves and blamed each other, each trying to jockey for position to avoid the worst of the allocation of responsibility and punishment.

It was approaching nine-thirty, with court due to start at ten, when their solicitor summoned the family in to meet the barrister.

'Good morning to you all. This is Mr Michael Lawson QC, who will be presenting your case in court.'

Mr Lawson carefully introduced himself personally to each of the family members and shook hands. April was reassured by the degree of warmth in his introduction. He explained his role and the format of the next few days. He carefully went through the charges in respect of each of the three defendants and confirmed that the family understood. He informed them that it would be stressful and emotional and that some witness statements would be used from Sam before he died, and for them to be prepared for that. He indicated that Kate would be on hand personally or available by phone at all times for more information or reassurance. Finally, he reminded them that he had a professional task to perform on behalf of the Crown, but must be dispassionate and remain rational in the interests of justice, although he would do his best to represent their interests fairly. With that, he rose from his chair, gathered his papers and moved towards centre stage. The solicitor said that Mr Lawson was a fine barrister with an established reputation in such high profile and complex cases. Their solicitor then had to leave to attend to other business.

The family were left with Kate before taking their seats in court.

'How are you feeling now?' Kate asked.

'Uneasy, but I suppose I just want to get on with it,' replied April, 'to get it over.'

'Yes, of course, understandable, but you must remember that it will not be quick. Also, that when you take your seats and the defendants are called into the dock from the cells, that will be the first time that you see them all again. Their appearance will be different – the long hair and beards were all false. They may stare at you in an attempt to intimidate you and they may have family members in court and they may do the same. No doubt their families have been fed a pack of lies and they will see you all as the enemy. If that becomes a problem let me know. Avoid any contact with any of their family outside and report it if they approach you. April, are you still sure that you can handle open court and don't want to use the screen?'

'Yes, Kate, I am,' she replied. Kate had reservations but accepted that it was April's choice.

She went through the charges with them again with a more detailed explanation.

'These are the charges after all due consideration by the CPS, and all the changes in circumstances: Charlie O'Toole: theft of paintings x 9 – estimated value of £3m; aggravated burglary; murder; rape x2.

'Danny Hunter (Dog): – the same.

'Jimmy Godfrey (Chaff): theft; aggravated burglary; murder (joint enterprise); rape x2.

'So, all are charged with the theft of the paintings, which might not stick. All are charged with entering your house illegally by force and destroying some of your property and taking it away (that refers to your mobile phones), which should stick. All are charged with Sam's murder, although Chaff didn't strike a blow but was complicit, therefore is charged with joint enterprise. The argument here will be whether the assault actually caused his death. All are also charged with double rape in the two different incidents, the first one being the more difficult to prove.'

'And if we win with all that, how long will they get?' asked April.

'It will largely depend if they get a straight determinate sentence or life. Life would mean that they cannot be released until they have served a minimum time set by the judge, otherwise if it is a determinate sentence then they will serve half of that sentence in custody,' Kate replied.

'OK, despite the technicalities, how long will that be?' responded Mark.

'Your barrister reckons time in custody could be anywhere from five years upwards. Could be a lot more, depending on how the trial goes, so we will have to see.'

Despite her best efforts the family felt confused; they had been told that sentences could be very long, now it could be as little as five years. They didn't understand.

The family hadn't really thought about their degree of involvement in the trial, simply that they were required to participate, but in the event, having built up some courage for this ordeal they felt that they were not centre stage at all. In fact they felt quite marginalised. It seemed to be all about the lawyers. Well read barristers in formal dress engaging in intellectual jousting and aiming to score points against each other. They obviously loved the theatrical aspect of it, but for the family it did seem like watching a play from the wings, and of course there was an awful lot of waiting. In fact, it was quite boring.
The first day went by without their involvement and it almost felt like a disappointment; like waiting to go on stage but never being called.

The first part of the trial was setting the scene and the context and then dealing with the first incident relating to the theft of the paintings. This didn't seem to go particularly well, with the defence being able to establish sufficient doubt, and Kate advised them that it could go either way.

In fact, it wasn't until the second week that the court even moved on to consider the hostage element of the case. For the first time, the family were then called as prosecution witnesses. Mark and Jan survived their first unequivocal one could be in attributing the cause of death in this way.

ordeal. It was very difficult for the family when Sam was mentioned. It all felt so academic and sanitised, but of course for them he was their only son. It did seem to be established, however, that Charlie and Dog had used the baseball bats against Sam, but of course it was only Jan's testimony that really counted, as she was the only witness to that event. The defence didn't attempt to deny that an assault had taken place. The medical evidence was that Sam's initial injuries were consistent with being struck by several blows from a hard instrument. Charlie and Dog both blamed each other and claimed that only one of them had struck Sam, and tried to minimise both the severity and the impact of the incident.

There was inevitably considerable argument about whether the blows could have directly caused Sam's premature death some time later. The pathologist for the Crown was very clear and seemed quite convincing that the initial level of injuries that Sam had suffered were serious, that the delay in access to medical treatment had in his opinion been critical and that the post mortem had indicated that the cause of death was a blood clot in the brain, which he felt was the direct consequence of the original assault.

'So, Doctor Patel, to be clear, if I am correct, in your view had the assault on Sam Hartwell in his family home not taken place, then all things being equal, he would not have subsequently died in the way or at the time that he did?' posed Mr Lawson QC.

'That is correct,' he replied.

The defence barrister attempted to cast doubt on this conclusion and to suggest that Dr Patel's relative inexperience had to be questioned in making such a critical judgement. The defence medical witness also added some weight to this argument in questioning how

Chapter Fourteen

Now the time had come for April to take the stand and give her evidence. The scene had been carefully set. Kate had gone over some basic coaching points with her again and April felt ready, as ready as she would ever be.

Mr Lawson checked with Kate before he left.

'How is she? Do you think she'll be alright?' he asked.

'She's alright, I think. I'm not sure how she'll do. I just hope she'll be OK,' she replied.

April had at least had some time to gain familiarity with the court setting and had dealt with the distaste of seeing the men again. In a strange way it felt different because they were not as she remembered them and therefore weren't as threatening. They were also contained in the dock, so couldn't touch her, and she felt able to face them. Their families in the public gallery, however, did look really threatening.

Mr Lawson described the lead up to the first rape to the jury.

'I want you to picture being a fifteen-year-old girl waking in your bedroom and hearing strange voices downstairs, then hearing people approaching trying to hide, being discovered and then brutally raped by two strangers. That was the ordeal that the two men known as Charlie and Dog put this poor, innocent girl through.'

He then started to question her, to build the picture; to give an impression of the fear, the confusion, the embarrassment, the horror and the pain, the indignity of one following the other, politely taking turns in stark contrast to the utter lack of compassion, consideration or humanity shown to her. He asked her how she felt at the time.

'It was like I was frozen, utterly powerless and alone. I was speechless; too scared to say anything in case I made it worse. I remember the look on their faces of total disregard for my feelings. It was all about what they wanted, and I had no doubt that they were going to take it. I just tried to think of something else, something nice and to wait for it all to end. I remember the smell of their bad breath and the smell and look of those horrible surgical gloves.'

'Can you tell the court what sexual acts they subjected you to?'

The sound of anticipation and shock echoed around the court as April took a deep breath.

'One made me do oral sex then they both raped me twice,' she said with her voice starting to crack and tears starting to roll down her face.

'Were you a virgin?' he asked.

'Yes,' she replied.

'Can you tell the court what impact this attack has had on you?'

April paused, tried to control her breathing and looked out strongly towards the jury. 'I lost my virginity. I was left bleeding and bruised. Subsequently I have had a series of infections and was made pregnant before having a miscarriage...'

'It's alright. Take your time,' Mr Lawson assured her.

'I have nightmares, feel low and don't want to meet people or do things. I have been so ill. I've not been at school and don't look forward to the future now. I still feel so scared.'

'Thank you. That will be all for now,' Mr Lawson said.

The court took a break and April went out to cry. Her mother met her, hugged her and said she'd done well.

The defence case rested on casting doubt that the first incident had happened at all, was just a figment of her imagination and that the medical evidence of sexual contact was less than convincing. From the family's point of view, the barrister whilst doing his job, lacked any compassion or feeling for his witness as he challenged her.

'Miss Hartwell, I put it to you that what you describe is nothing short of a pack of lies; fantasy; the wild imaginings of a furtive young woman. These men did not rape you, nor did they assault you.'

This was too much for April and she broke down in floods of tears in the witness box, before regaining some composure to reply, shaking, crying with anger and disbelief. 'That's so easy for you to say, sir, but you weren't there! These two men,' she said firmly, pointing across the court to Dog and Charlie, 'came into my room and ruined my life! They know they did! Just look at their faces!' she cried directly to the jury.

Jan and Mark were questioned on April's appearance and demeanour after the incident. Nothing could be scientifically proved in this instance – it would be left to the jury to form their own opinion, which in many ways was the strength of the jury system, Kate assured them.

At the end of the day, the family gathered exhausted in the witness room to hold each other, to share the pain, to try to sustain and to endure. Kate joined them and tried to add to the sense of mutual support and comfort as Mr Lawson entered the room flamboyantly with his gown flowing behind him.

'Well done today,' he said with sincerity. 'You all did well and came across honestly and consistently. April, I was so proud of you; you were truly marvellous!' he exclaimed as he removed his wig.

April blushed. It was a warm and encouraging sign for all of them that through it all, in blushing she had in fact maintained some of her youthful innocence.

Chapter Fifteen

As the family emerged from court the media were still waiting, taunting, sensationalising; in short, just being their usual insensitive and sensationalist selves.

This aspect of the whole experience was often one that victims found one of the most difficult to deal with, Kate reflected. Not only were their lives changed forever by gross intrusion, but suddenly they also became public property. Most victims were completely unprepared for this she had found, and were often quite overwhelmed by it, compounding their sense of injustice and isolation.

Mark, Jan and April had no energy left for this rabble and barged their way through to the waiting police car to take them home. Kate had used the rear exit from court and collected her car having anticipated the mob.

When she had taken them home Kate could sense that all the family wanted was some peace and some space, so she left promptly. It was such sensitivity that was one of the reasons why Kate was so good at this specialised role. She was a mature officer in her fifties with more than twenty years experience of police work, including working with the Vice Squad in the Metropolitan Police. She had seen more than her fair share of the seedy side of life. Her dark hair and quite stocky if not frumpy appearance didn't attract undue male attention. She was, however, very astute about what made men tick. She could also both weigh up and reassure in equal measure.

Kate also had a dark secret that she rarely shared with anyone. She too had known the pain of victimisation.

She had never married and never had children. She had always lived alone, shunning close relationships after being raped at school by her male PE teacher who was the coach for the netball team. She was only fourteen years old. At the time she had not been believed and it had never been properly investigated. It was something that she didn't dwell on, but nevertheless some residual pain and injustice remained. She felt that at times it helped her understand and that it helped motivate her to seek justice for others.

Back in the cottage April collapsed on the sofa and that distant, vacant stare returned. She glanced sideways to see her mum and dad share a brief peck on the cheek as they both left the room. She was pleased that they seemed to have found each other again; it had helped the general atmosphere in the house. She missed Sam at times like these, when his casual sense of humour would lift her mood. Sam was tall and strong, quite athletic really. He had competed at quite a high level in various sports whilst at university. April wasn't sporty. She had aspired to go to university and had wanted to study science. She felt she wasn't bright enough to become a doctor or a vet, but fancied studying something vaguely medical. Now she couldn't even take her GCSEs. The tears returned again. Where would this all lead? she wondered. Her English teacher had stuck to his promise to see her at home and to encourage her to at least pass her English exam. She wished that other teachers had been so kind, but then wondered if she would have the energy to participate. She didn't really know what she thought anymore. Just take things a day at a time, had proved to be a good maxim for now.

The doorbell rang. April didn't feel like visitors at the moment so headed for her bedroom.

'Darling, its Lucy from school come to see you!' announced her mum hoping that it would cheer her up, knowing that Lucy had tried to stay in touch. April felt fairly neutral. So it was Lucy.

Lucy asked how she was and said that her friends missed her at school, but April sensed that there was more to the visit. The two girls went into April's bedroom and chatted, catching up on school news and things. The distraction of normality for a moment was actually quite liberating, to think of bands and concerts and who was going out with whom; who was cool and who was naff.

'April, there is something else,' Lucy confessed eventually. 'Have you been on Facebook recently?' she asked.

'No. Why?'

'Well, it's just that some people have, well, been a bit nasty really,' she said.

'Come on, Lucy, what do you mean?'

'Well, do you remember when you snogged Adam Maples at the school Christmas disco last year and someone took your photo?'

'Yes,' she said, starting to feel anxious.

'Well it's been posted on Facebook. People have seen your court case reported on television and some of the boys have said that you must have been good, so now that you know what it's like they'd like to go with you, too. That's all,' Lucy said uneasily now that she'd let the cat out of the bag. 'It's only boy talk, April. I thought you should know, that's all,' she said trying desperately to achieve some sense of damage limitation.

April just didn't know what to say to yet another example of crass insensitivity from people she thought were her friends.

'Lucy, it's not your fault. Please, just tell them it was horrible...the whole episode...that's all...' April spluttered out eventually. How could people be so cruel? And these were people she knew well, she thought. 'Why can't people understand?'

Lucy didn't know where to turn and didn't think telling her that her brother had bought a new mountain bike or that she had been shopping in Oxford Street was going to cut it. 'I'm sorry April, I really am,' she said limply. 'Had I better go?'

'Yes, I think so.'

Lucy left her with an attempt at a reassuring touch of the hand, but even with her tender years she knew full well that it was not enough.

'Goodbye, Mrs Hartwell,' she said as she left the house.

After Lucy had left, Jan went upstairs to see April, who was crying.

'What was that all about, darling?' she asked.

April struggled to tell her, struggled to confide in her but tried.

'Oh dear, darling, I don't really understand this face box thing...'

'Face*book*, Mother!'

'Oh yes, sorry dear,' she replied, feeling inadequate and recognising the limitations of her sometimes clumsy attempts to connect with April. She thought of Kate. Might she do a better job? Jan wondered.

'Darling, do you want me to ring Kate and ask her to talk to you?'

April paused, sighed then reflected that maybe her mother could even be right and that this wasn't a bad idea. 'Oh, do what you like; call her if you want!' she stuttered, hoping that she would.

'OK, darling, I'll ring now,' responded Jan, not sure if she was doing the right thing.

Kate arrived promptly and sat and talked with April for over an hour. Kate shared some of her own experiences and tried to reassure April that she was not alone. April responded and Kate could read some sense of appreciation through the barriers of teenage angst.

Jan saw her out and tried to show some empathy, as Kate explained that sometimes social media can be so cruel.

*

As the court came alive, April was preparing for her next ordeal. Today she would be questioned about the second rape. Both Kate and Mr Lawson had offered reassurance that her feelings of apprehension were perfectly normal.

Mr Lawson had again set the scene for the jury and was explaining that it appeared, for whatever reason, that Chaff opted to stay in the house when the other two left to try to escape via the track leading towards the footbridge.

April had explained that she had asked to take a shower before the men moved out of the lounge, then when she came out of the bathroom Chaff followed her into the bedroom and removed her towel, leaving her standing naked in front of him.

'And he proceeded to do what exactly?'

'He raped me...twice.'

'Did he use force? Were any words exchanged?' he asked calmly.

'Yes, he had a knife and held it towards me. I didn't know what he might do.'

'Go on.'

'But he carried on and raped me...and...and...I remember asking why? He slapped me and carried on again. I didn't expect him to stop, although I wanted him to stop, but I just remember thinking...why are you doing this when you can clearly see my distress? Why?'

'And did he give you an answer?'

'No, not really. Not that I remember.'

'Thank you, Miss Hartwell.'

April paused and gathered her strength and as the defence barrister rose to his feet she could feel her anxiety rising.

'Miss Hartwell, are you expecting this court to believe this story? I ask the court, would the defendant known as Chaff have realistically stayed in the house rather than try to escape with the other two men? Whatever the court decides about culpability, whatever else these three men were, they were not fools! I put it to you, Miss Hartwell, that the truth was more that you actually suggested that he stayed. That you asked him to stay and that you inferred to him that you would make it worth his while. Having imagined the first alleged incident, you went one step further and actually propositioned my client, inviting him to have sex with you. Yes, you did have sex with this man. We know that, there is medical evidence, but ladies and gentlemen of the jury, the question I must pose is: was that sexual act consensual? Well, Miss Hartwell, was it? Am I right?'

Gasps went around the court and Jan and Mark were holding hands so tightly as both were struggling to control their emotions.

April drew breath and this time with no tears, replied, 'No, sir, you are not... I have suffered such indignities, cried so many tears, that no, I did not invite this man in any way or suggest anything to him whatsoever. He forced himself upon me, twice, and left me bruised, infected with his disease and pregnant... No, sir, I did not ask for or invite this to happen.'

April was standing firm, holding the old wood that surrounded the witness box in an old style court room that held so many memories, a court room that could tell so many tails. She was shaking, but standing firm, looking the barrister square in the eye and doing her best to tell it how it was – no embellishments, no vindictive added elements for good measure, just the plain, simple, honest truth. She hoped that she would be believed, and that was all that she could do.

By the close of the day, Jan was still livid about the defence barrister's line of attack. She wanted to challenge him about it afterwards, in fact she wanted to do more than that, but satisfied herself with expressing her raw emotions to Kate in private in the witness room.

'Kate, how can that man say such things?' she demanded.

'How can it be right in a court of law to allege that my daughter, aged only fifteen at the time, somehow decided to offer herself to a man she had never met until he forced his way into her own home, beat her brother literally to death and left her injured and pregnant? It's ridiculous! Its more than ridiculous, actually, it's quite obscene!' Jan cried out.

'I know. I know,' said Kate calmly. 'I agree, but this is theatre, as I warned you...'

'Yes, but theatre of the absurd!' Jan countered.

'OK,' said Kate trying not to laugh, as she didn't think it would help in this instance. 'I like that! I did try to tell you that this would test the outer boundaries of your tolerance and beyond, but he is only doing his job. Actually, he's representing what the gang would say, and in that sense 'ridiculous' is really quite useful.'

Jan looked pained and unconvinced.

Kate continued, 'You perhaps didn't see the looks on the faces of the jury. I can tell you straight that they were horrified, too, by the suggestion and were impressed with April's response. Actually, I have seen quite a few tears from the jury, too. April is doing so well. You just have to trust that they will do their job, too.'

'I suppose so. Incidentally, Kate, it's just occurred to me, why would such callous men be so accommodating in allowing April access to the shower?'

'They knew she'd be washing away the evidence, I'd expect.'

The trial moved on. The barristers both questioned the defendants, during which they blamed each other, changed their stories and lied with apparent ease. Sitting in a position of relative comfort observing the proceedings, the Hartwell family all agreed that the defendants had made a poor start and that the jury did not seem impressed.

After more legal argument it finally came to closing speeches from the barristers. Mr Lawson said that he liked this part of a trial and was feeling fairly confident. He spoke with ease, turning towards the jury frequently for emphasis and dramatic effect. He outlined the major planks of the prosecution case, referred to the relevant evidence and concluded that all three men were thoroughly guilty of all charges. The only difference between them being that Chaff's association with Sam's murder was by joint enterprise alone. He painted a human picture of the impact of the whole saga on the family and the likelihood of long term effects, particularly for April. He emphasised her youth and that no one could underestimate the impact of loss of innocence in such a violent manner. He presented his case well, with clarity and conviction. The family felt satisfied that he did a good job.

The defence barrister made the best of what he had to work with and emphasised the relative weakness of the evidence in relation to the theft, and tried again to undermine the connection between the assault and Sam's death. He went on to maintain that the first rape was a figment of April's imagination and that the second incident represented consensual sex. The mood around the court was not going his way.

It was coming to the end of a long day in a long process and everyone was feeling jaded. It was left to the judge to make his final remarks to the jury. He made it plain that theirs was a serious responsibility, furthermore that they must consider the evidence and not be swayed by emotion. He advised them on the law and that their conclusions should follow from their interpretation of the evidence.

After all that had happened, the result of the case against these three men lay in the hands of twelve members of the public to decide whether they were guilty or not. It did seem odd that this remained the case after all the various professional involvement that had taken place. Kate advised the family to relax. Given the number of charges, she anticipated that the jury would not deliver their verdicts quickly, in fact it may well be tomorrow.

Jan suggested coffee and the three of them visibly relaxed several notches while Kate made them all drinks. Not much was said but there was some sense that they had come through the ordeal of the trial and had survived.

Chapter Sixteen

The members of the jury retired to their allotted room to consider the vast amount of information they had heard over the course of the trial. Not untypically, none of them had taken notes and all felt some sense of the weight of responsibility placed upon them, as they tried to remember everything, something, anything. Over the course of the trial they had little opportunity to actually talk to each other and for some it felt like a lonely experience. Neither had any of the jury members seen each other outside the court setting. They knew very little about each other's lives before this chance meeting randomly threw them together. Nor, of course, did they know what their different reactions to the task would be. In fact they were not permitted to discuss the case at home or outside the court and this had been more of a strain for some than others.

Their first task was to elect someone to chair the proceedings and announce their verdicts. That privilege was soon decided once a tall, imposing, quite serious looking gentlemen opened the debate and reminded them all that this was their first task. He was immediately nominated. A bright younger professional woman was also invited but she was happy to defer to the older gentleman. That decided, there was much shuffling and coughing as they settled down to their task.

'I suggest that we look at each of the charges in chronological order against each of the defendants. Remember we have to be logical, not just intuitive in making our decisions. The strength we have is in numbers. If all of us, or at least a majority of 10 to 2 believe that they are guilty, then they probably are,' announced their newly appointed chairman confidently.

'Well, I reckon they are all as guilty as sin!' announced one lady immediately. 'To think what they put that poor girl through. And the lies! Unbelievable! I'll tell you what, I've met some bad ones in my time, but these three men are positively evil! Hang 'em all, I say!'

'OK, well we will all have our views, but before we get to that let's at least try to review the evidence,' said the chairman diplomatically. 'In relation to the painting theft, what do people think? It wasn't entirely convincing was it?'

'All guilty, and that's all I'm saying', said the same lady. 'Do you realise she was only fifteen?'

A rather studious young man attempted to raise the level of debate. 'It seems to me that the descriptions of the four men who casually lifted the paintings are so similar to the four men in the Hartwell family's house that it is entirely plausible that they are indeed the same men. Also there was one matching fingerprint, do you remember?' There were nods. 'And it looks like the plan was to lift the paintings and move them on, possibly via the inside man, while our gang of four looked for a bolt hole to wait for things to calm down. Whether they had already identified the Hartwells' house, didn't seem clear to me, but the time and distance seemed reasonable if they wanted to put the authorities off the track, I remember thinking.'

'Um thank you,' responded the chairman. 'Does anyone agree?'

'And she was a virgin! I ask you!' added the lady indignantly.

The professional looking young women added, 'The paintings theft does imply some planning, inside knowledge, extensive contacts and, well, a degree of intelligence. I'm not convinced frankly that these three men would be up to it. They all seemed terribly dim to me.'

'They all have form, as they say, don't they?' added another member.

'Yes, I have their previous convictions here,' said the chair. 'The three men in court all have form, as you put it, but nothing in this league.'

'How about the fourth member? Perhaps the fact that he hasn't been caught suggests that he was the brains,' said another.

'Well, if they didn't do it, why hold up at the Hartwells'? That wouldn't make sense. They didn't really make much effort to steal anything and it didn't look like they knew who was living there, so if they didn't know about April, then they didn't go with the intention to rape – it was opportunist,' said the professional young woman.

Another member added a comment. 'I'm retired now and a grandmother. I don't know about these sorts of things and frankly was struggling to both hear half of it and to keep concentration, but in my mind they did it. Call it women's intuition if you like, but I have no doubt, like the first lady.'

'I'm a self-employed builder and I'd rather have been at work, particularly now in the busy summer period, but I wasn't too convinced about the theft, though as you say, why go and camp at the Hartwells'? Anyway, will it make much difference if they all go down for murdering that poor young lad, let alone what they did to that young lass?'

'Yes, and she was only fifteen you know!' repeated the first lady, again.

The debate continued. When it became obvious that they were not going to reach a verdict that day, proceedings were suspended and the jury were moved to a hotel for the night. Although they had all been warned of that, nobody had really thought about it or made any preparations, and there were plenty of mutterings about children and husbands' tea until someone reminded them what this was all about. For the family it just prolonged the agony.

The following day the jury resumed their work early. They decided to move on from the theft and to consider the other charges. First they asked themselves if they were they all satisfied that entering the house, given all the circumstances, constituted aggravated burglary. Much as the debate about the paintings, they agreed that the answer was no, not really, but the overriding feeling, despite the technicalities, was that the men were guilty.

In respect of the murder, they were far more convinced and decisive – there were no voices of dissent. They all agreed that in assaulting poor Sam with baseball bats they had caused his death, and despite it being not entirely clear who exactly hit him, all three men were present and no one attempted to stop it, so they felt that they were all guilty.

'We must now move on to consider the rapes,' said the chairman sombrely, expecting a further interruption from the first lady, but on this occasion there was none. 'I suppose it boils down to who we believe, April or these three men?'

'Well I think she was entirely believable, the medical evidence speaks for itself, poor girl. Being raped is bad enough, but several times by different men, being infected, getting pregnant and then having a miscarriage must have been just awful. And frankly the story that it didn't happen and that she gave him the come on would have been laughable if it wasn't so tragic,' said one member.

'Yes, but you know what young girls are like these days,' said another lady.

'Yes, there's a young girl down my street whose only sixteen and her mother says that she's having sex all the time!' said another.

'But we are talking about this specific case and there was no suggestion that April was at all sexually active before this incident. She was just an innocent schoolgirl.'

'I agree,' said the builder. 'That story about her coming on to them was sheer bollocks, excuse me!'

'And she was only fifteen!'

Time passed before the chair interjected. 'Well, does that about seal it then? Are we all agreed? They are guilty in relation to both rapes,' he said in an attempt to sum up. There were sober nods all round.

'Is that it then?' asked a young mum. 'Can I go now? I'll just catch the next bus.' Sharp looks from several quarters suggested not.

'So, what about the paintings?' the builder reminded them. 'As I said, I don't think it will make much practical difference, but in for a penny? I'm happy to throw the lot at them!'

The mood around the room was sombre and calm, other than some fidgeting by those who were more interested in reaching an end than concluding in the interests of justice. There was recognition that despite what the builder had said, it probably did matter, at least to the family, and especially to April, that they were guilty on all counts. They were also all aware that she was so young. They reminded themselves that the consequent sentencing was a matter for the judge and that their task was to look at each charge in turn.

The message was sent to the usher that they were ready and the news quickly circulated around the court. All the key people involved started to take their seats in eager anticipation of the jury's return and the delivery of their verdicts. The defendants and their families just hoped that they had all managed to blag, confuse and cast sufficient doubt to walk away relatively lightly. For the barristers and court officials it was an issue of professional pride, but for the family it was solely about truth and justice. Not vengeance, not even punishment, but about an open acknowledgement of what had actually happened to them, what they had lost and who was responsible. Sadly, for some members of the jury at this point, it was just about getting home.

The court settled. The judge looked down from his lofty position and uttered the time honoured words. 'I understand that you have reached your verdicts?'

The chairman of the jury rose to his feet and answered in a clear and confident voice, 'Yes, Your Honour, we have.'

Each defendant was named in turn and the charges against them read out. In relation to all three men the jury had concluded that in relation to theft, aggravated burglary, murder and rape the verdict was one of guilty on all counts.

There were gasps and shouts around the court in equal measure. For the family this was vindication. This was another vital step along the road to recovery. This brought at least the prospect of putting this behind them. For the barristers there was the inevitable sense of success and failure respectively, and for the defendants crushing reality and trepidation about the sentences to come.

The judge allowed the court to come to a natural lull before regaining a sense of decorum.

'Ladies and gentlemen, I thank you all for your participation throughout this most difficult of trials and I have decided to reflect overnight on the proceedings and pronounce sentence in the morning. I bid you good night.' With that he rose and retired and the court began to clear.

*

The family returned home managing to avoid too much contact with the media circus outside. Their solicitor was left to make the usual fairly bland statement reflecting the family's relief and their wish to be left alone now. DCI Goodwin also made a brief statement thanking the witnesses and all her team for their hard work and dedication. She concluded with a robust message.

'Let this case send out a clear message to the criminal community that if you perpetrate such serious crimes, the authorities will be relentless in tracking you down, and the courts will deal with you most severely.'

'How long can we expect the sentences to be, ma'am?' asked one journalist reflecting the mood of the pack.

'That's entirely a matter for the judge, but I expect they will be substantial,' she replied diplomatically.

The family felt relieved, but most of all they all felt exhausted. It had been a long ordeal with their lives effectively on hold until now. Only now could they dare to dream, to look forward, to plan, to regain some control. Their lives had changed forever; they had lost

Sam, their lovely family home was to be sold and they were left to pick up the pieces feeling very alone and quite vulnerable.

Mark had been wondering whether he could face returning to work having lost so much time and momentum and was thinking that he might opt for retirement. April still hoped to take that English exam but hadn't thought any further than that. They sat round the kitchen table with a cup of tea and just stared into space. The moment was in one sense unnerving, yet almost therapeutic.

The silence was broken by the phone ringing. A series of calls followed throughout the evening from well wishers. Whilst none of them felt very sociable, there was some comfort in the fact that others had at least recognised their plight. Whilst acknowledging the concern, none of the family felt that they had the energy to respond, but felt that they must.

Chapter Seventeen

The morning brought one last official hurdle with the pronouncement of sentence about to start. The court was calm and subdued. The offenders' family members and supporters looked broken.

The barristers took their seats and Kate ushered the Hartwells to theirs. Each of the family members exchanged glances, contemplating the range and intensity of emotions that had accompanied them to this point – emotions that were unwelcome and uninvited but that could not be ignored. Feelings that were transient, feelings that would last, but for this moment most of all a sense of uncertainty and expectation prevailed throughout the court room.

'Kate, I suppose we will lose you now, now that it's all over?' asked Jan.

Kate answered with as much reassurance as she could, knowing that in many ways their journey had now only just begun.

'No, I will stay in touch for as long as you want me,' she said, and hoped that her DCI would agree.

'Court rise!' called the usher.

It is usual for the sentencing judge to summarise the case before passing sentence to give a rounded account of the context and the courts findings. These statements are used afterwards for many years by those who work in criminal justice in an attempt to get that message across to the offender and in both risk assessment and assessment of progress. The comments made at this time tend to be stark and these were no different.

His Honour, the judge walked in and took his substantial seat at the head of the court, as the room fell silent.

'Good morning. Firstly I want to acknowledge the work of the authorities in this case and the strain placed on the Hartwell family. I am going to address my comments to all three of the prisoners in the dock.

'In over thirty years of working in the legal profession this is one of the most heinous crimes I have had the displeasure to deal with in it's depth of sheer depravity, callousness and brutality,' the judge remarked as the prisoners visibly shrunk a little more into the dock.

'As a gang of four men, with inside help you steal a substantial collection of highly valuable art treasurers then seek to evade police attention by hiding up in the family home of an unsuspecting group of law abiding citizens. You,' he said, gesturing very clearly to the prisoners, 'then proceed to brutalise all four members of the Hartwell family. You savagely assault young Sam Hartwell, leaving him severely injured and deny him medical treatment, causing his eventual death.'

Tears began to flow as he continued.

'You take over this household, plunder it of all sustenance, hold the occupants captive and then when you discover an innocent young girl you brutally and systematically rape her, robbing her of her virginity, infecting her with your vile diseases and making her pregnant. Whilst two of you try to escape, one stays behind to impose further indignities and tries to use that same innocent victim as a shield to barter his freedom. Well I can tell you all that you failed! You have presented this court with a pack of lies, blamed each other and offered implausible explanations riddled with inconsistencies. You have shown not an ounce of compassion or remorse throughout the whole proceedings! It is my duty therefore to protect the public from wicked men such as yourselves by using my powers to ensure that you stay in custody for a very long time.

'I find you all guilty to the same degree in relation to rape and only differentiate slightly between the three of you in relation to murder – both offences attracting a life sentence, murder being mandatory and rape being within my discretion.

'Charlie O'Toole and Danny Hunter, on the counts of murder and rape, I sentence you to life imprisonment with a requirement to serve a minimum term of thirty years.'

Gasps rang around the court as the prisoners shrunk yet further still into the dock.

'On the count of theft, I sentence you to fifteen years, and on the count of aggravated burglary to ten years, both to be served concurrently.'

Sighs, gasps and tears echoed through the court as the assembled audience attempted to absorb the significance of what they had just heard.

The judge continued to hand out the same sentence to Jimmy Godfrey, save a tariff of twenty-five years with murder being considered as joint enterprise.

'Take them down.' With that the judge rose as the court stood in stunned silence and he left to reflect on his work in the privacy of his chambers. Most of those present looked both pleased and supportive towards the family. Not even the offender's supporters could raise a grimace after such an address.

The prisoners were returned to the cells as sentenced men, no longer on remand, but to be dispatched to different high security jails to start their sentences. The court probation officer would have to interview them all individually to test their reaction and to warn the receiving prison of their attitude and demeanour.

The family chose to sit awhile in the witness room and take stock before facing the world. Various officials walked through to offer their best wishes, including the judge.

Kate explained the sentences to them again.

'Basically, all three have a life sentence with no prospect of release for two of them for thirty years and twenty-five years for the other one. The fifteen and ten year sentences are theoretically served at the same time. Joint enterprise incidentally, means that the third man also bares some responsibility for being part of the process although he didn't actually strike your brother. After that it's up to the parole board to decide if their risk is manageable in the community. They'll all be well into their fifties by then and they may never be released, so you have no need to worry.'

After all they'd been through, at that point in time it did sound very reassuring.

PART THREE

THE RECOVERY

Chapter Eighteen

After all the drama and tension of the trial, the first few weeks following the event felt quite boring by comparison and were quite an anti-climax. The whole journey had been so all consuming that it really felt to the family like they had to restart their lives almost from scratch.

However, as they tried to do just that the Hartwells were faced with regular reminders that they were not free of officialdom.

Kate had told them to expect a letter from the probation service offering contact with the victim liaison officer, if they wished. When the letter arrived it explained their right to know restricted details of the progress through sentence of the offenders in their case and to have some say in later deliberations with the parole board in granting any future release. At this point it all seemed too nebulous, too far away and too painful. After a short discussion they all agreed that they didn't want to reply. At this point they just wanted to leave all that behind, and any thought of being informed of eventual release of these evil men just wasn't something that they wished to contemplate.

Mark's firm agreed to his retirement and all his work mates told him that he was doing the right thing. For a small private firm the package wasn't bad and Mark was actually feeling quite excited about getting some control back over his life.

Jan wasn't sure where these developments would leave her and indeed their marriage. She felt that Mark had probably assumed that he had done more than enough recently to ensure that their relationship was back on track, but Jan still had her doubts. Yes, he had in fairness been very good recently but his actions during the hostage period kept coming back to her and were difficult to forget...and to forgive. In the short term she busied herself with domestic duties; cleaning the rented cottage, cooking nice meals and generally looking after her flock, but was that really enough? she thought.

Between them all, the family decided an early task would be to hold a memorial service for Sam. His funeral had been a bit of a blur for all of them and they felt that they wanted to remember him properly; they owed him that. Kate thought that this was a good idea. She had diligently kept to her word, without being intrusive was always there for them as required and kept in touch well beyond the call of duty.

For April things were very different however. She wasn't looking for a peaceful retirement after all. She still had her whole life in front of her and wanted to expand her horizons, including experiencing the good things in life. She had managed to take and pass her English exam, but any further aspirations would require further study and probably a return to full time education. After all that had happened and the head teacher's general attitude she wasn't at all keen on rejoining the school even in the 6th form. In fact she didn't feel very motivated at all. Kate was gently trying to encourage her to access counselling and start to try to deal with recent events, but again April was not keen. This was not the right time, she felt, she just wasn't ready yet but she didn't really know what she wanted as an alternative.

April still felt very weak and run down by her recent experience and was having nightmares and difficulty sleeping. Her GP, Dr Bajek, had been very supportive throughout, and again was trying to encourage her to put some structure back in her life. Her mother couldn't help making suggestions, many of which were unwelcome. Jan felt that a distant relative should emerge and offer her daughter sanctuary in somewhere like the Austrian Alps for six months, breathing good air and getting plenty of rest and reflective time, a bit like what usually happens in the Famous Five stories when any of the characters needed recuperation, but of course real life wasn't like that.

Jan also felt in need of some respite and had suggested that she and April could go away somewhere together. She thought it might even provide a useful opportunity to have some space and time away from Mark, but April hadn't shown any enthusiasm for this idea either.

April just felt a lack of energy and motivation and little interest in things generally. Getting back on track and thinking about her future just all seemed too much. Everyone was telling her that it would take time, but she didn't want to wait. She wanted to feel better now.

Further correspondence seemed to drag them back into the mire of criminal justice. None of them had even thought of the whole area of appeals, and being confronted by this new dimension came as a devastating shock.

'What's this?' shouted Mark. 'I can't believe it! We've gone through all this and it ended – they were locked up – and now, so soon, they want to 'appeal' – run the trial again? I don't understand!'

'Let me see, dear,' said Jan, equally concerned and confused.

They looked aghast at the letter and cried together before seeking reassurance from Kate. They were to learn that effectively no court decision was final and that the three convicted men would each try to persuade eager lawyers, keen to take the work to seek holes in the case; claim the discovery of new evidence and seek to amend or overturn their convictions or reduce their sentences. No matter how spurious these attempts seemed, they continued – and at public expense.

It was to prove to be a painful and recurrent sore as far as the family were concerned. Kate did her best to try to put things in context for them, as did their solicitor, but the pain and the reminders seemed so unfair.

Chapter Nineteen

Lucy from school rang.

'Hi April, how are you feeling?'

'Pretty crap really,' she replied.

'I know it must be really tough. I did follow it on the news but didn't want to bother you. I told the boys how horrible they'd been and they did say sorry – a bit anyway. Aiden still fancies you, by the way!'

'OK,' said April with disinterest.

'I just wondered if you knew that there was a house party at Jack Turner's arranged for tonight. His dad has let us use one of the barns. We can make lots of noise and stay late! Jack's brother has brewed a keg of beer and Samantha is bringing some of her dad's cider. Just bring a bottle if you want to come. It's anytime from eight onwards. Most of us are going to sleep in the hay. I'll give you a lift if you want. It's going to be wicked!'

'Thank you, Lucy, that's really kind; I appreciate it. I'm not sure. Don't make any plans for me, but I might make it, I'll see.'

Part of her wanted to go; part of her thought that it would probably do her good. She also knew that her mother would say that, but part of her just couldn't be bothered.

Jan came back from shopping and asked how April had been and received the same flat answer as usual. All Mum had talked about since Sam's memorial service was how nice it had been and how kind everyone was. April was tired of it. It was as if for Mum that was enough, she thought. No, that wasn't fair, but April was sure she'd rather have Sam back.

'April, darling, your father and I are nipping out for supper this evening with the Jacksons. It will be lovely, I'm sure. I've bought a selection of those ready meals you like so you'll have a choice. I've also bought you some ice cream for afters. There's some pop music programme on TV tonight darling, so I'm sure you'll be just fine.'

April cringed. Well that's it then, she thought, a microwave dinner watching my mother's selected crap, or a night out and get wasted. No contest! So April rang Lucy back, arranged the lift, found some horrible cheap plonk in the garage that nobody would miss and started to think about outfits and stuff. She realised that she hadn't been 'out' for months and didn't know any of the craic about who was with whom. She almost felt excited.

A few hours later, Mum shouted upstairs, 'Bye, darling, got to rush – the Jackson's are such sticklers for time! Just five minutes in the microwave, darling – don't forget to pierce the film,' and the door slammed and she was gone. She assumed this included Dad, but didn't really know, nor much care.

April emerged in what she thought was a suitable outfit to relaunch her social life: a short skirt, but not too short, with black leggings and flat shoes and a colourful sparkly top. She bounced out of the house with a key, her mobile phone, a few tissues and the cheap plonk.

Lucy's mum was giving four girls a lift to the farm. The mixed smell of perfume in the car was almost overwhelming. Conversation flitted quickly from music to boys to films and back to boys, with lots of laughter and shrieks of girlie excitement.

When they arrived at the barn all the occupants rushed out leaving Lucy's mother alone in a car with three out of the four doors left wide open. She tutted, got out to close them and drove off.

The party was great. It did April good to get out and meet her friends again. People were kind and said they were pleased to see her but she could sense that mostly they felt awkward and didn't know what to say, so opted not to mention the obvious. April moved around between groups, enjoyed a drink, the company and the music.

Lucy felt how exciting it was to be out. 'April, this is great and I can't wait to sleep in a barn!'

April agreed that it sounded exciting but didn't know how she would feel about trying to sleep with others so close by.

They chatted and drank and danced for a while. Time seemed to be suspended and irrelevant. It was dark and it was fun. April began to just feel young and even carefree again. As drink took over and the conversation became sillier, April noticed that groups and couples were forming and there was a drift from the barn dance floor to the hay loft. She felt a little uncomfortable and unsure. One of the boys suddenly appeared next to her, put his arm round her and went to kiss her. She did quite like him and responded to his invitation as they embraced, but she felt ill at ease. He then took her hand and led her into the hay, where they rolled and kissed and cuddled.

As he got more excited April felt more uncomfortable and the memories of her bedroom came back – the smell, the gloves, the intrusion, the pain. Whilst she wanted to just let herself go and enjoy the moment with Max, she didn't feel that she could and suddenly felt tense. He was attempting to run his hands over her shapely body and to navigate his way around zips and straps and fastenings, but she rolled away. He followed but was sensitive enough not to persist as she started to cry. He guessed why, as some of the other girls appeared to support her. April was so disappointed, she just wanted to enjoy it, but felt that she couldn't. Those men had spoilt it and she felt that she was back in the house, trapped, feeling abused and powerless. She sobbed as Lucy regained some dignity from under the hay and took her hand to lead her away for a moment.

The two girls sat and Max was kind enough to find some water and then made some coffee as they talked and tried to help, but for April there was the growing realisation that overcoming her recent experiences was not going to be either quick or easy. She felt frightened, anxious and quite alone. Is this how it is going to be? she wondered. Is this what I've been left with?

Chapter Twenty

In the morning after a round of frantic phone calls between mothers as they discovered the absence of daughters, a series of cars began to arrive to recover the dishevelled girls. Jan had agreed to collect the four girls that Lucy's mum had driven there the previous evening. Not much was said as handbags, shoes and items of clothing were gathered and mobile phones secured to return to their world of mass communication – games, apps and Google.

The girls were quiet in the car as they politely reported to Mrs Hartwell that it had been a pleasant evening and they had all slept well in the girls section of the barn and that their arrangements had drawn to a close at around midnight.

Meanwhile in another car, four boys were boasting about their conquests and how great it had been to stay up until four, as one of the dads asked, 'Planting wild oats then, boys?' as he drove away from the farm. His son thought, What? Silly old bugger, we were shagging in the hayloft! Or at least that's what they told each other.

Back home, the atmosphere was subdued as Jan attempted to say all the motherly things about telling her in advance, letting her know where she was, coming back at a reasonable hour and being 'careful'. April replied with all the daughterly responses of 'What's it to you? Why do you want to know? And oh my god! You are so old fashioned!' as she sulked, slammed the door and disappeared into her bedroom, not to emerge for several hours.

Over the next few months this pattern continued, with April gaining superficial confidence and going out more, whilst her parents were trying to encourage her to return to full time education or get a proper job rather than the few casual hours she was working in a shop. April was becoming more subdued and confused. Kate had kept in touch but was starting to drift away, and despite Dr Bajek's invitation and encouragement, April was not motivated to engage with counselling or to say very much. She was keeping her thoughts to herself, generally ignoring her own feelings and starting to turn her anger on herself.

It was at this time that April first met Wayne at one of the parties. He was twenty-five and she felt attracted by his charm and 'maturity'. He had a nice car and started to take her out with his older mates to nightclubs and restaurants and to see live bands in concert. Mark and Jan were concerned and didn't regard Wayne as a good influence, but the more they tried to talk to April about it, the more she resisted and they risked driving her away. They began to notice that she sometimes looked glazed and was becoming more distant and more subdued.

Jan tried to talk to Kate about it but found it increasingly hard to contact her. She gave up after a while when she learnt that Kate had been transferred to other duties and wasn't involved in witness protection anymore. Mark struggled to deal with it, preferring to try to ignore it, none of which helped their relationship, and again they started to drift apart. He spent much of his time with his mates either bowling or in the pub. Jan was feeling increasingly isolated. She hadn't really invested in making her own friends over the years but had played the supporting wife to Mark with his business contacts and got involved with the children's activities and their friends. Now she was beginning to regret that approach as she found herself less needed and more alone. Jan had never been much of a drinker but now she was gaining a taste for gin and drinking more of it.

Mark had arranged to go away for a week with his mates to play in a bowls tournament. April couldn't face the prospect of being at home alone with her mother in her ear all the time so made an excuse to stay with Wayne for the week. She told her mum that the shop had asked her to cover another store in London and that they would provide accommodation for the whole week, and Jan had bought it.

In time April had overcome her initial unease and anxiety about sex, but she still didn't really enjoy it. She wondered whether it was just her role to provide pleasure for men. The thought crossed her mind many times that maybe the gang were right about what they said in court and that she was just a little tart and that she had led them on. She didn't know. She felt confused. But she was looking forward to spending a week with Wayne.

Wayne was waiting to meet a customer in London. The man was often late, but was a reliable payer. He worked in the City in some capacity, Wayne thought. He was certainly well dressed and presented, and bought the best products at a premium price, so he was prepared to wait. He sat in his usual seat in his favourite pub near Marble Arch reading the paper. Ten minutes later the customer arrived and pleasantries were exchanged. Business was duly transacted and they went their separate ways.

Wayne later met up with his mates, Curtis and Abdul.

'So when's that little piece of yours coming over for the week then, Wayne?' asked Curtis.

'It's next week, mate,' he replied.

'Nice,' said Abdul, with a glint in his eye.

'She is seventeen now isn't she Wayne? We don't do kids!'

'Yes of course she's seventeen. She'll be good. She's just another runaway. That girl raped in that house – it was on the TV news. I met her at some party and saw potential. I'll keep her sweet and I reckon she can earn us some money.'

'Yeah, I'm sure you're right,' replied Curtis.

*

Mark left the house for his short break. They were still renting and hadn't felt that they had the energy to sort out another house yet. Mark was driving his big 4x4 and set out to pick up the other three men. They then set off for the tournament on the south coast. In their own ways they all felt glad of a break. Alan worked in a high pressure job, Jed was just recovering from cancer and Colin had recently lost his wife. Each had their story to tell and looked forward to sharing their experiences and seeking the support of old friends. The tournament therefore was a chance to relax and enjoy each others' company. They had booked into a nice hotel and had secured a good deal with a full breakfast, packed lunch and dinner.

The first day was supposed to be a relaxed introduction with an opportunity to test the greens and be briefed on competition rules and expectations. They were surprised that it was so formal. The competition was organised in three events at three levels, and being relative novices, the four friends had opted to start at the bottom. They had no gauge to measure the likely standard of competition. They wanted to enjoy it and didn't take it too seriously. In fact they didn't take it seriously at all! After the first day they gathered in the bar for a few beers before dinner.

Mark's phone rang and it was Jan, again. He chose to ignore it, pushing it deep into his pocket and letting it ring.

'Isn't that your phone, Mark?'

'Yeah, it's just a nuisance call. Forget it.'

They remained in the bar after the first day's play. Things had gone well and they had enjoyed each other's company.

'So, here's to a successful tournament!' they said, raising a glass. The first day had been just practice and briefings for the rest of the week. They had entered the third competition at beginner level and hoped to do well on their first experience of such an event.

At home Jan was getting worried. She had noticed the preparations April had made to go to work away and it didn't look right. She had been vague about the details, and when Jan had asked for the address of the shop, April had dismissed her request saying she didn't need it. 'Oh, just use my mobile, Mother, if you really must contact me!' she had said indignantly, as she left wearing enough makeup to start her own shop.

Jan wanted to talk to Mark about it, but he had warned her that the signal wasn't very good in the area where the tournament was held.

By day two, Jan's suspicions were growing as she cleaned April's room and found receipts and cash point slips jammed in a drawer, and quite a lot of new clothes in the wardrobe. She tried to call Mark again but got no reply. She rang April, but her phone was switched off.

Jan decided to do some shopping to distract her anxiety and she could call into the shop where April worked to check the arrangements and ask for her contact details. This offered her the prospect of some reassurance as she left the house.

Jan went round the usual supermarket with little enthusiasm with no one to cook for or look after. Her trolley looked so light, she thought, as she added another bottle of gin. She laughed to herself as she selected three more microwave ready meals that she said she would never sink to but now had to acknowledge that she had.

After packing her single shopping bag into the car, Jan set off to walk to the shop where April worked. They had been good to her throughout the trial and afterwards in accommodating a varied work pattern, and she was grateful. She felt that she knew all the staff quite well by now.

As she entered the shop she was met by surprised looks as she approached the counter to enquire which branch April had been posted to.

'Oh, hello Mrs Hartwell; how are you? I'm surprised to see you,' said the shop manager.

'I'm fine. I was just wondering if you could tell me which shop April is working in this week please, she forgot to leave me the details.'

'I'm sorry, Mrs Hartwell, but April doesn't work here anymore. I had to let her go over a month ago. She had become too unreliable. I'm sorry, we did our best for her, but we couldn't keep ignoring the fact that she didn't turn up. I thought you knew.'

Jan was devastated. This confirmed her worst fears. Not only was April drifting away, but she was lying to her and she felt powerless to stop it. The shop manager could sense her distress, but couldn't really help and just felt embarrassed.

Jan slipped away, sharing the sense of unease. She held it together as far as the car and on the short drive home, but collapsed in tears as she entered the house. What have those men done to my family? she wondered. Jan had always been so together, always the strong one, but suddenly she felt so vulnerable. She wanted reassurance; she needed Mark, but he wasn't there. She stumbled to the phone and rang, but it rang out. She put her head in her hands and sobbed. Her son was dead, her daughter was going off the rails and now she and her husband were growing apart again. What's happening? she thought. What's happening to us? She reached for the bottle and poured another large gin.

Mark and his mates were enjoying their game. They had done well on the first day's full competition and were learning as they went along. Some of the teams were so serious and so intense, they had to laugh. It was only old man's marbles after all, they thought. As they left the green Mark checked his phone again and found that he had three missed calls from Jan. He thought he'd better check in. The others went back to the hotel for some tea and he rang home.

'Jan, it's me. Sorry I missed your calls, what's wrong?' he asked, hoping it would be nothing, but all he could hear was gibberish, between tears. He really couldn't make much sense of it.

'Jan, come on, just calm yourself; I can't hear you properly. Tell me what's upset you.'

Jan tried to compose herself and explain, but the best she could manage to say was to ask him to come home. 'Come home, now Mark, please!'

Mark was still trying to work out why she was so upset. He sensed that she was drunk and suggested that she should go to bed and he'd call in the morning. He offered to ring and ask a neighbour to call in, but couldn't make any sense of her reply. He thought best to do that anyway. It was four o'clock in the afternoon and she sounded legless. He didn't really know what to think, but decided that to rush home now would be the wrong call. He returned to his mates.

'Everything alright, Mark, you look a little troubled?'
'No, I'm fine, just answering a call.'
'Who from?'
'Oh, no one in particular,' he replied dismissively

*

April arrived in London and found her way to the pub near Marble Arch where she met Wayne. He smelt of beer and had obviously been in there for a while as he met her with an enthusiastic kiss and a grope of her bum. April just accepted it.

Wayne had some friends with him for her to meet. That was kind, she thought. He introduced Curtis who he said worked in the fashion industry and Abdul who was a photographer. How exciting! April was impressed. They bought her drinks and talked about opportunities in modelling, complemented her on her appearance and made her feel special. April had grown by now into a fine looking young woman with strong facial features, bright blonde hair cut in a bob style and she had a good figure. She was enjoying the attention. At last these were people who appreciated her for who she was, she thought, and talked to her like an adult. They were so kind they didn't even mention her circumstances at all.

After they left the pub Wayne took her for something to eat and then back to his room in a shared house. He said he just used it as his London base and that his own house was out of town.

Wayne made the opportunity to have sex and filled her head with hopes and dreams about fashion, modelling and success...and she took it all in.

*

In the morning Mark rang Jan before the day's bowling. She felt dreadful and apologised for her behaviour last night. The neighbour had called round while she was being sick and helped her to bed. Jan felt embarrassed, she wasn't used to booze and she'd never been so drunk before. Through the haze she was still worried about April though.

'Mark, I'm so sorry, I've made such a fool of myself. I feel so stupid,' she said.

'Don't,' Mark replied, while thinking that he agreed with her. 'It happens; you'll get over it,' he said with less than convincing sympathy.

'I'm still worried about April though, darling, she hasn't come home. She told me that she was working away, but that's not true, I checked with the shop. I don't know what she's doing! She could be anywhere!' cried Jan, starting to get upset.

Mark couldn't help feeling that this was an over reaction and wasn't too concerned, but tried to sound interested. 'Jan she has probably gone with a friend, or maybe she is working away with a different shop and didn't tell you that; you know how secretive she has become. She's a young woman now Jan, you have to learn to let go.'

'Are you coming home?'

Mark didn't know quite what to say. He couldn't see the need and didn't want to leave his hard earned break with his mates so early in the competition. He also wondered what in practical terms he could do even if he did go home. 'Jan, I really can't just leave at this point. I'll stay in touch – we've found a place where the signal is better,' he said lying, but thinking on his feet. 'I'll listen out for your calls and ring in the evenings. Let me know if there is anything you want me to do,' he said limply, as the others signalled it was time to go.

Jan felt alone. She had been married a long time and Mark had been OK, he had been a good provider, but other aspects were missing. She knew he saw things in practical terms, but she just wanted some support. Really she just wanted him there, but again he was absent when she needed him.

'OK, boys, I'm with you, let's go!' Mark shouted.

'Who was that, trouble at home mate?' asked Colin.

'No, just a wife that's suddenly discovered the link between alcohol and hangovers!' Mark replied.

They laughed. 'At our age!' responded Jed. 'Must have led a sheltered life!'

'Yes, she has, or she had,' replied Mark quietly.

The four men carried on with the game. Day three was due to be the crucial stage to determine which teams would get through to the next round and to the finals tomorrow. They laughed as they rehearsed famous sporting lines and tried to get into 'the zone'.

*

The following day April was excited at the prospect of meeting Curtis and Abdul again to further explore her modelling potential. She hadn't thought of a career in this industry, but thought that at her best she had something to offer. She looked in the mirror and thought, not bad, hey! She could feel her confidence returning.

Wayne offered her some toast and said they would eat properly later. He looked excited, too. She felt a little dopey and hoped that Wayne's strong coffee would pep her up, but it seemed to have made things worse.

They drove into the City in Wayne's big flash car and April felt like a princess, looking out of the window at the passing crowds. They arrived at some sort of studio, which looked quite posh. She was impressed. Wayne was being so nice to her. Curtis was there too, looking very stylish.

'Wow! You certainly know how to dress!' she said.

'Good morning, April, we are all ready for you.'

'Great!' she said before finding the loo.

'Have you given her something, Wayne?' Curtis asked.

'Yes, just a small dose; we can top it up later if necessary.'

'OK, this way,' Curtis said confidently, as April emerged from the toilet having freshened up her make-up.

They walked into a photography studio to meet up with Abdul who was lining up various cameras.

'Right April, Wayne has done his bit now and will be leaving us shortly, so just listen to Abdul and we'll take some preliminary shots.'

'OK,' she said. 'What about different outfits? Surely I'm not OK just dressed as I am?' she asked innocently.

'You'll be fine, love. It's just a preliminary shoot. You are keen to make it into fashion aren't you? And you know that means certain sacrifices, don't you?'

'Oh, yes,' she replied with enthusiasm, 'I'm sure it will be worth it!'

'We hope so, yes,' said Curtis slightly coldly.

April went in front of the cameras and responded to Abdul's instructions. She posed and she pouted. She let herself go and felt that she was actually quite enjoying it, although she still felt a little light-headed, almost like being drunk. As his instructions got more explicit she almost didn't seem to notice, or to care. She felt again that maybe this was her role, her destiny. The shots got ever more revealing and intrusive, by which time April felt frozen. In her mind it was almost like being back in the house – she could smell the images again and it felt almost like an extension of that same experience. Abdul took lots of photos and said he was pleased with the results and that she had done well. No further mention of a fashion career was made and Wayne was no longer there.

She still felt woozy as she got dressed and they told her that she was free to go, that they would be in touch and that they had her bank details for payment.

As April walked outside she looked for Wayne, but his car wasn't there and she realised that he had never given her his latest mobile number as he had promised. She also thought that she couldn't remember actually where he had taken her, where that room was. She looked down and the small suitcase that she had brought with her was propped up against the wall where Wayne's car had been.

What now? she wondered, as she suddenly realised how hungry she was and how tired she felt. April felt confused. Where was Wayne, she thought, where am I now? She felt embarrassed, but that she could hardly crawl back home now. She wandered along the road for a while, trying to get some bearings, but nothing was familiar. She stopped by a bus stop and looked around her for road signs, shop names, anything to give a reference, but there was nothing that helped. Then a bus came and impulsively April stepped aboard.

'City centre, love?' asked the driver.

April nodded and paid the fare. She sat down and just looked out of the window as the bus continued on its route. She wasn't sure where she'd been or where she was going, except that it was new and that it wasn't home.

April got off the bus by Euston station and wandered in looking for something to eat. She ordered a large burger and fries in the nearest café and a large coffee to try to wake up. It didn't take her long to consume her meal and she soon started to feel tired again. She walked back into the main body of the station and found a bench and sat down. Despite the noise and general level of activity, she quickly fell asleep.

'Are you alright, miss?' asked one of the railway security staff after she had been observed sleeping for several hours.

'What? What?' she replied, waking suddenly and expecting to see those men, those abusers standing over her in her bedroom. But she was not back in the house, not back in that horror. She looked around and recognised a railway station and started to remember where she was. She couldn't remember much about getting there, but she could sense where she was now. April looked up at the kindly black face in front of her.

'I'm just checking that you are OK, miss. We've noticed you have been asleep for the past four hours and have kept on eye out for you on CCTV from the control room and we thought it was about time I came to check you out. You sure you're OK?' he asked again.

'Yes, yes, I'm fine, just tired that's all. What time is it?' she asked

'It's four o'clock, miss.'

'In the afternoon?'

'Yes, miss. Have you got somewhere to go, miss, for tonight, or are you travelling home?' the man asked, recognising her vulnerability from dealing with countless runaways at the station over the years.

'Yes...I'm staying with my aunt,' April replied, unconvincingly.

The station security guard sensed her uncertainty. 'Well, you just look after yourself, miss, and be sure to ask for help if things don't work out,' and he handed her a card with some contact numbers for services for the homeless.

'Yes, yes, I will,' she replied, looking round for the loo.

'It's that way, love; go on I'll watch your stuff for a minute,' he said, knowing it was against the rules, but wanting to help.

April was grateful for his kindness, thrust the card into her pocket and headed for the toilet. Afterwards she thanked the man and started to walk off, out of the station and into the unknown world outside.

Sitting on another bench Jonny had been watching them and got up to follow.

April walked slowly, not really knowing what she was going to do next. Traffic was flashing by and people rushed past in all directions, all seeming to have destinations in mind, plans and deadlines to meet. April had none of these things. She wandered along aimlessly until she saw a café on the main street and walked in to get a cup of tea. What now? she thought again. She still felt slightly woozy, but strangely calm, taking this in her stride almost as if it wasn't her, but someone else. She thought of home. She thought of Sam. She wondered if her parents would stay together after all that had happened. She wasn't sure. April didn't really feel sure about anything. In fact she just felt numb, neutral.

Jonny was nineteen and had lived on the streets for four years since leaving Newcastle. He didn't miss his abusive father or his alcoholic mother, only his dog,

Mac. Jonny had long straggly hair, knotted and dirty. He smelt. He carried his few things with him as he walked around during the day. He survived – a bit of begging here, a bit of shoplifting or street robbery there. Sometimes he was lucky and the rich tourists didn't even notice as he lifted a handbag or wallet from in front of their eyes. He followed April and he waited.

April finished her tea and left, returning to the street and to continue her aimless journey to nowhere. She passed several shops, a newspaper seller, a man in a doorway and a group of Japanese tourists with not a thought. Time was beginning to roll on and she began to wonder where she would go; where she would spend the night. She suddenly became aware of someone's presence beside her and turned to see a young man with long unkempt hair.

'Hi,' he said, 'I'm Jonny. You look like you need somewhere to stay. Come with me.'

*

Wayne returned to the studio, having done some more deals. These City bankers were so keen to spend their undeserved bonuses, he found, mostly on top end stuff, cocaine usually, and it was like taking mobiles from kids.

Abdul had processed the images of April and was getting on with their distribution to a variety of internet sites and publishers. The internet sites were the easiest money, they just wanted sexy images and would pay well, and promptly. The publishers, however, sometimes wanted stories to go with the pictures. Abdul had become good at writing such deceit: Victoria from Buckinghamshire wanted some variety from the attention of the stable lads in the family livery... Amy from Milton Keynes had applied for X Factor twice before, but this year was confident... Petal from London had a taste for naturist holidays... and so on. Popular crap, but he had become good at it.

'How did she do?' Wayne asked.

'Fine.'

'Worth using again?'

'No, I don't think so. We've got what we need.'

'OK, the usual fee then?'

'Yes, OK. I'll send her a couple of hundred quid. Then she can't complain.'

'Right, and we make the usual thousand or so?'

'I should think so!'

The two men were pleased with their day's work and took no time to consider the damage that they were doing.

Chapter Twenty-One

Jonny led April through the streets, away from the City centre, beyond the facade, into the other world. As they entered the squat April could sense the depravity, the smell, and the tension. Jonny took her past dirty mattresses, piles of old blankets and dog litter through to another area in the rear of the old industrial building. Used needles were scattered across the floor. At the rear of the building the sun appeared through a hole in the roof letting in a shaft of light. This area seemed quieter and there was less indication that it was occupied. April felt a slight sense of disquiet. Was this a safe haven or was it going to lead her into more trouble? she wondered.

'You can use that one if you like,' offered Jonny. 'He was arrested in town this morning. He won't be back for several months, I shouldn't think.'

April looked down at a pile of cardboard with two blankets on top that did actually look new and probably were, as the wrapping and high street store labels seemed to confirm.

'Um, he must have been expecting guests!' said Jonny.

It was early evening. They had picked up a sandwich on the way and sat down to eat it. Jonny handed her a fresh bottle of water from his stock by his bed space. They began to talk as other activity unravelled around them. April sensed a couple having sex in the far corner, someone throwing up further back in the room, another man urinating by a wall and a woman and child crying somewhere in the distance. This is really quite Dickensian, she thought, and giggled that her English teacher would be impressed. April wasn't sure whether this was a game, a test, a threat or what it was. Only that for now, for this moment, it was her existence. Jonny seemed kind, as he started to talk of his life back home.

For the first time since the incident April started to feel relaxed enough to want to start talking about her experiences. Jonny listened as she explained and described what had happened in the house. With tears in her eyes, April went on to describe the rapes, the trial and events since. Jonny had heard many stories of human tragedy and depravity during his time in London. Nevertheless her story touched him. Jonny tried to keep his eyes open for the vulnerable while he was out and about. He reasoned that in his state no one would give him a job, so he tried to justify his criminal activity by balancing it with actions of humanity, assisting other young people in need and trying to keep them away from the clutches of those who would seek to harm them. He had met many such youngsters over the past four years, some as young as nine or ten, most of them in their teens. Escaping abuse, drink, drugs, gangs, bullies and hopelessness were common reasons for running away. He just wished that there was more provision for such people but he knew that there was not.

They sat and shared a roll up and some more water. Jonny said that he didn't drink. He had seen it do too much harm, but he did like to smoke cannabis. He was sympathetic and April felt a real sense of relief at having shared her burden with somebody. Maybe the doctor was right, she thought, maybe counselling would help. She asked Jonny.

'So what becomes of all these damaged people then, Jonny?'

'Well, sadly some commit suicide, some fall into the clutches of even more devious monsters, but some do seem to find a way out of it.'

'Do you think counselling helps, Jonny? My GP suggests I should try it.'

'I think it's very middle class, April. Did you say that was your name?'

'Yes,' she replied.

'Sure, it can work for some, but you need somebody you can trust, and that may not be easy to find. Too many well meaning amateurs in my experience; nice middle class people who have never seen anything of the seedy side of life. They are too neat and only see things in conventional terms. You need somebody who has been there, at least to some degree – I think so anyway,' he said softly.

They continued to talk about families and school, lack of opportunities for young people, sex, drugs and how they might climb out of this mess. April felt some form of bond with this young man. She knew that she would only stay one night and that she could hardly take his email address or write to him, but she wondered what would become of him.

As torches flashed around the old building, and people coughed and dogs barked, April tried to get some sleep. She didn't fear any risk from Jonny, but was very uneasy about the rest of the inhabitants of this awful place. It was a very restless night. April was frequently disturbed. The baby that she heard earlier cried from time to time and she could hear people moving through the building.

She drifted off again then woke to see the shadow of a man looking through her bags. Jonny woke and shouted for him to move away. He scurried off like an animal. She thought she saw a rat follow him into the dark corners of the building. After that April couldn't sleep and just tried to keep warm as best she could. The light was starting to come through the hole in the roof, as was the rain. It was uncomfortable. In fact it was disgusting.

After another hour or so drifted by, April rose from her cardboard bed and wanted to move out quickly. Jonny stirred and offered to help her out through the building. She felt grateful as they rose to view this awful place again. She felt clammy, itchy, nervous and confused as they moved away and left Jonny's part of the squat. After some predictable cat calls she quickly emerged from the back of the building along a short cut that Jonny knew and back onto the streets, back into the facade of respectability.

Before they parted April remembered the card that the guard had kindly given her and pulling it from her pocket asked Jonny if he had heard of any of these services. He said that he understood that the women's refuge south of the river was a good place, and with that she left him to return to his reality with a sense of unease. After all, she did still have some attachment to her previous world, which she presumed Jonny no longer had with his. For a moment she felt sorry for him for his circumstances and grateful for hers. Jonny had been kind and she waved goodbye wondering what would become of him and accepting that she would probably never know.

Her phone was still working and she rang the number of the refuge that Jonny had endorsed. As someone answered the phone she could hear a host of activity in the background and children crying. The female voice just said 'Hello, can I help?'

Jenny confirmed it was the right number and April explained her circumstances. She egged it up a little saying that her parents had rejected her and that she couldn't return home. After some further questions, including how she got the number and where she stayed last night, April was invited to visit and given the address. She didn't have much of a clue where it was, but really wanted a shower and a chance to collect her belongings and thoughts together, so opted to take a taxi and use her last few pounds, reasoning that at least the driver would know the address.

As the taxi stopped outside, the refuge looked like a normal big house in a city street, if a little scruffy, but nevertheless inviting. With some trepidation, April rang the bell, spoke through the intercom to confirm who she was and entered as the door was opened for her electronically.

The refuge was chaotic, but welcoming. April was offered a bed for the night in a bunk in a small cramped and slightly smelly room with six other young women, two with young children. Jenny took a few more details from her and showed her through to the communal room where tea and coffee were available and women and children were enjoying sanctuary.

April looked around. There were all sorts of women here; different ages, races, and attitudes. Many different languages were being spoken and yet there seemed to be a sense of peace and a connection between the occupants. She guessed that some would be escaping from similar circumstances as her own, but she didn't know. This was all new to her.

Her attention was sought by a little Asian boy who held onto her leg and smiled. She guessed he was about two years old. He appeared to be bruised on his face and was unkempt. Despite this he had an engaging smile.

April leant down to greet him and he held out his arms. As she lifted him up he smiled broadly and giggled as she swung him round. Once in her arms, he wouldn't let go and she carried him with her as she accepted a cup of tea and sat down to try to make sense of what was happening.

April desperately missed Sam at moments like this as her feelings of loneliness and isolation returned. She missed his company; a brother to bounce ideas off and help her cope with her mother; a confidant, a friend. April and Sam had always been close and despite what had happened to her, losing Sam was in some ways far more difficult to take. He was young and had so much energy, so much more to give, and now he was gone.

As she pondered her loss, the little boy in her arms attracted her attention again. He snuggled close, trying to lose himself in her embrace. She pondered that he helped to remind her that life does go on even in the most deprived of circumstances and that life is unpredictable, taking different and sometimes unexpected twists and turns. She dwelt on her situation, trying to take stock while she lulled the child to sleep. She regretted being so abrupt and dishonest with her mother and wondered how she might bridge that gap. She wondered about Wayne and how she had allowed herself to be abused again, if indeed that was what happened – she wasn't sure. The sense that she was somehow to blame haunted her. April felt that she hated herself, then the thought went through her mind that at least she had been promised some payment, but that didn't make her feel any better, in fact it added to her sense of guilt and self-loathing. Then she wondered whether payment would ever arrive or whether that too was a trick. Confusion reigned in her mind.

April wondered about Jonny and how he would cope and how many people there were out there living in those circumstances. As she looked up an Asian woman approached her holding the hands of two other small children with several others following along behind.

'Ah, here he is! He looks very contented. Do you mind?'

'No, not at all. Looks like you have your hands full; I'm happy to hold him.'

'Thank you,' she said, as she smiled and moved away.

'April, I see you are making yourself useful, that's good,' remarked Jenny, as she invited her into a side room with her bundle. 'Let's have a chat and see how we can help you.'

April followed and sat down. Feeling an immediate sense of support, she started to cry.

'It's so hard, Jenny; I'm only seventeen and feel so alone! I'm in a desperate mess and don't know what to do!'

'Come on, tell me all about it – we have experience of dealing with all sorts of problems here,' said Jenny with calm reassurance.

April started to tell her story and felt some relief in being able to express it. Jenny listened, made no judgements and held her hand as she cried. She had heard the account of many rape victims, but this was extreme, unusual, and even she was shaken by the apparent callousness of her attackers. She allowed April the space to just let her tell her story. To express it was an important step forward to help release some of that emotion, the anger, the pain, the sense of injustice. The rawness and confusion inherent in April's account was all too evident to Jenny. In her experience, rape victims often took years to be able to remember or describe events and put them into any sort of perspective, let alone begin to move on. Being at just the beginning of that process she feared that April had more chaos to go through yet before any thoughts of recovery could even begin.

'April, well done. I think that's enough for now, you need to rest. Why don't you go and lie down and get some sleep for a while together with this little boy? I'll pop in to check you are OK in a few hours,' Jenny suggested reassuringly, and April gladly acquiesced.

Jenny was left to deal with her own feelings of sadness, disgust and the temptation of sinking into disillusion. This was not unusual and she managed to use those emotions to strengthen her resolve to help the April's that she met all too often accessing their overstretched service. In this case she felt that was going to be especially hard.

After some rest, Jenny suggested that April's mum would be desperate to hear from her. To hear that she was OK, and despite recent events to know that her daughter was safe would be far more important than whatever was said before she left. April knew that Jenny was right, but still didn't relish the prospect of a call home. Nevertheless, she breathed deeply and made the call.

'Hello Mum, it's me...' she said tentatively.

'Darling, I've been so worried! Where are you? What happened? You mustn't worry about a thing!' Jan replied, trying to alleviate all her anxieties at once.

'Oh, Mum, I'm so sorry. I've been such a fool!'

'Don't worry, it doesn't matter. Are you safe? Where are you?'

'Yes, I'm safe. I'm staying in a women's refuge in London.'

'...OK, well whatever, just come home, dear, just come home!' pleaded her mother in desperation. Why London and why a refuge? she thought, but was more focused on just reaching out to her daughter. Having lost a son, at that moment Jan felt that she would have done anything to secure the safe return of her daughter.

'I'm not sure, Mum,' April replied. 'Honestly, I'm OK, but I need a bit of space. I need to think.'

Jan knew it would not be wise to push too hard at this point, but still felt intensely worried and wanted the reassurance of a contact number, wanted to ring the refuge herself, but knew that it was no good. As Mark kept reminding her, April was effectively an adult now and had to go her own way. Jan guessed that no refuge would disclose details of its residents in any event.

After the call ended, Jan collapsed in a heap of nervous anxiety on the sofa and sobbed. It was so hard having lost Sam, and now feeling that she was facing seeing April drift away and being powerless to influence events.

Mark had returned home. As he came in from the garden he immediately sensed more upset. He drew back from saying anything critical and tried to be reassuring, placing his hand on his wife's shoulder, but she turned away.

'Mark, Sam's gone, now we are losing April!' she shrieked at him. Mark didn't know how to react and decided it was best just to leave her be for a while, and after offering to make some tea returned to the garden. He wondered how much longer he could stand this tension.

Chapter Twenty-Two

April stayed at the refuge for several days before being referred on to a voluntary project. In the meantime, payment as agreed did appear in her current account for her brief experience of 'modelling'. Enquires, however, soon found that the source was untraceable to any individual, let alone 'Wayne', and April hadn't the energy to pursue it any further. The refuge staff assured her that she was not alone and that the police in their experience wouldn't investigate it without far more details than April could provide. Wayne was probably already on their radar and would get his comeuppance eventually, Jenny assured her.

April learnt that the voluntary project, 'Blue Skies', offered supportive housing to young single women in South London. Jenny thought that it would be more suitable to April's needs as the refuge was more of a crisis reception centre and the Blue Skies Project would offer more structured support to help April adjust and start to think about her future. Following a visit, April agreed and moved the short distance to begin a new start. It was odd, she thought, how things can happen. One day four men had arrived and her life had changed forever, but since then she had encountered some random acts of kindness from people like Jonny in the squat, the security man at the railway station and Jenny at the refuge. She found that helpful – it put some perspective on just feeling 'done to'. Shit happens, as they say, but nice things can happen, too.

She was offered a bed in a shared room in the project assessment house, where all new residents began their stay. After some initial reception procedures April was allocated a key worker, helped to apply for benefits and signed on at the local doctor's surgery as a temporary patient.

April's roommate was Amy, who was from Australia and had got into some trouble whilst travelling across Europe. The two young women felt a connection straight away, which helped them both to settle in, and they started to share their stories.

'How long have you been here, Amy?' April enquired.

'In the UK or in the project?' Amy replied.

'Well both, I suppose.'

'April, I came over here last summer as a gap year student before planning to go to university in America,' Amy explained. 'I flew into Greece initially and worked in restaurants and bars whilst travelling across Europe. I arrived in the UK a month ago and ended up here yesterday.'

'Wow! What an experience!' April replied, feeling both humbled and impressed.

'And you?' enquired Amy.

April explained some of her recent troubles and family history. The girls got on well, chatting for hours and enjoying each other's company. It helped April express some of her anger and Amy to share some of her frustrations with the international authorities.

It transpired that Amy had been robbed whilst travelling across Europe and had her cash, cards and passport stolen. She had been exploring alone and the loss left her in a very difficult and vulnerable position. She was, however, quite resourceful and had managed to persuade a beach restaurant to take her on for a month.

They provided food and accommodation and the chance to earn enough money to phone home and sort out replacement cash, cards and insurance claims. The whole process had seemingly taken an age to resolve to reasonable satisfaction. However, the loss of the passport proved to be more difficult to address. A series of frustrating and complicated encounters had unfolded. Various European and Australian bodies had tried to verify her status and establish an acceptable address to send on a replacement. Without the valid documentation, Amy had effectively found herself feeling trapped, unless she chose to cross Europe and risk not needing a passport at any time. Whilst free movement within the EU was supposedly accepted, she had found that a passport remains a vital document to prove your identity and legitimacy.

When it did eventually arrive, all her outline travel plans had overrun and had to be either cancelled or rearranged. Amy had coped with that but when she arrived in the UK she was immediately identified and retained by the authorities. It appeared that her stolen passport had been used by criminal gangs to aid smuggling operations and drug dealing. She had been released on bail whilst the authorities sought to satisfy themselves that she was in fact the real Amy Morgan. The Australian embassy in London had been helpful at least to the extent of suggesting some ideas for suitable accommodation to avoid either a remand in custody or being held in a deportation centre. The Blue Skies Project had been prepared to offer her an address, which had been accepted as suitable whilst enquiries were made, before the police had released her yesterday.

Over the following few weeks the two young women spent much of their time together. April found Amy's spirit of independence inspiring and helped to give her a sense of hope. Amy, for her part shared some concern and sympathy for April and her plight, and wanted to help. Amy had seen her share of trouble and chaos both back in Australia, witnessing domestic violence at home, as well as the various problems whilst on her travels. She had learnt to survive, sometimes stretching the boundaries in some risky circumstances. She had learnt how to assess people and situations and see opportunities. Amy had also learnt how to manipulate men and avoid being used by them. Those tactics had helped her in her journey of discovery. Travel, she had found, was an education and an opportunity to just be herself. Things had not always gone her way however, as her recent troubles illustrated, but Amy generally seemed to come out smiling. She was a strong and positive character and just the sort of person that April needed to be around at that time.

Whilst sitting in a bar late one evening, Amy was conscious that the two girls were attracting attention.

'See those two guys over there, April, giving us the eye?' asked Amy.

April hadn't noticed. 'No. Sitting where?' she asked naively.

'Don't look round, but the two guys on the bar stools by the entrance have been eyeing us up for some time. What do you think?'

'About what?' asked April, turning just enough to glance at them and gain a reaction.

'Come on! I know you've had a tough time with men, but don't rule out some fun. Some guys can be cool, you know! How about I call them over?'

April wasn't sure, but in the wake of Amy's confidence, nodded enough for her to take the initiative.

With practiced confidence and relative ease, Amy turned her head and looked over her shoulder, smiled and signalled an invitation to join them.

Amy was slightly built and of modest stature, but had striking long reddish ginger hair and a warm and welcoming smile. The two guys couldn't believe their luck as they looked at each other and tried to appear relaxed, but were falling over themselves with anticipation to respond to this unexpected invitation.

They swaggered over. Introductions were made and corny lines exchanged as Amy led the conversation and weighed the guys up. Flattered, keen and harmless was her assessment, as she allowed them to try to impress and buy some drinks. April managed to relax enough to join the conversation and seemed to warm to their company.

The lads were up for a laugh and a good time and prepared to spend some money on a night out that showed unexpected promise. They explained that they were business executives staying in London for a few days before flying to Paris for their next assignment. April responded and was interested to hear more, but Amy could see through their attempt to impress, although was prepared to play along.

She changed the subject and asked if they knew any decent clubs in the area. Jack, who was actually a delivery driver from Kent, knew the area well and soon described a range of local available options. After a few more drinks they moved off arm in arm in two couples to enjoy an evening of loud music, expensive warm beer and drunken bravado.

By the early hours it was time to move on and Amy suggested going back to their place. Staying guests were of course against the rules, but she reckoned they could be discreet and that their accommodation was probably better than the guy's business hotel that she rightly suspected didn't exist.

With painful high heels the girls strutted back to the project whilst the guys scoured the stark urban environment looking for somewhere to have a piss. On arrival, handbags were ruffled, keys were found and ingress made. Coffee was skipped in favour of drunken fumbling before the guys made their excuses and left before dawn with a warm feeling and an empty pocket to return to their vans in a lorry park a few miles away.

In the morning April felt a little confused and guilty, although she had enjoyed the evening and the experience. For Amy it was familiar territory. April was able to talk openly to Amy, which helped her to gain a more balanced perspective about men, sex and relationships. On this occasion she didn't feel used and had willingly enjoyed the encounter – and that for April was healthy.

Chapter Twenty-Three

Several months had passed, and back in the rented cottage Mark and Jan were considering separation. Their drift apart now seemed too entrenched, too deep and too difficult to bridge.

Jan was in a state of emotional turmoil. She struggled to grieve for the loss of her son, was constantly worried about her wayward daughter and didn't feel that Mark was capable of easing her pain. She wondered whether he could provide the love and reassurance that she felt she needed at that time.

Mark felt that he had tried to accommodate his wife's moods and tantrums but that his reserves of patience, tolerance and love were exhausted. He accepted that some time apart was probably the best solution and realistically the only viable option left. The fact that the rental agreement on the cottage was shortly up for renewal had prompted their discussions. When Jan had approached the lease company they had said that there was interest from a large corporate customer for a five year lease on the cottage at a good price, and that the owner wanted to take it. As they discussed options, it became apparent that the company had a number of flats available in the area for both rent and purchase and that was the necessary impetus.

'Did you see the leasing company today as you'd planned, Jan?' asked Mark.

'Yes, in fact I did.'

'So what did they say?'

Jan sat down and began to cry. Many tears had been shed since that fateful night when four men had arrived on their drive, invaded their lives and turned them upside down. She explained the conversation and the options.

Mark remained standing; upright, aloof. 'So if we relinquish the lease here, we could rent two separate flats; is that what you are suggesting? Is that what you want?'

Jan was sobbing. 'I just think we've grown apart, Mark, the gap's too wide now. I just feel I need my own space.'

Mark had been thinking along similar lines for a while, but didn't want to broach the subject for fear of the likely reaction, so in a way he was pleased that it had come as Jan's suggestion. He didn't feel inclined to try to persuade her otherwise. He felt that he had tried his best and that his efforts had been largely unrecognised and unappreciated, but agreed that the gulf was now too wide to bridge.

It represented a sad end to a long established marriage, but in the chaos of the aftermath of recent events, both Jan and Mark with some reluctance accepted that separation had become inevitable. They decided that as the housing market was beginning to rise again they would be best to purchase rather than to rent. Both felt committed to friends and to the area and were not opposed to being near yet apart, so they purchased two flats in different developments with the proceeds from the sale of the family home.

After the pain of decision the momentum of action proved to be positive for both of them, and at the point of separation they both felt more than just resigned to their chosen path. It potentially represented new beginnings for each of them. Jan remained desperately concerned about April, whilst Mark was more relaxed about accepting that she needed to find her own way to recovery.

Jan explained the moves to April over the phone, but at that point she wasn't really listening. April felt that those men had already destroyed her family and that this was just another part of it. She felt numb. It wasn't that she didn't care, but more that she felt she couldn't engage with any more upset. April had effectively closed off emotion to a large extent, as a defence mechanism, and couldn't deal with any more. The only person she really opened up to was Amy, but unfortunately all that was about to change.

*

The police investigation into Amy's identity and the existence of two passports had revealed a pattern of extensive criminality. The investigation had proved to be complex but in trying to separate various strands the senior investigating officer was not satisfied that Amy was entirely innocent and not connected to the criminal gang or even the theft of her own passport. These were important matters and the SIO was excited about the prospect of bringing down some serious players and in doing so didn't want to risk Amy remaining at large and potentially contaminating the evidence or indeed attempting to leave the country.

At five o'clock on Monday morning the peace and quiet of the project was shattered by a heavy police presence when Amy was arrested. Across London similar operations were taking place to round up as many players and associates as possible to aid the investigation and hopefully lead to some significant convictions and lengthy sentences.

The authorities had no trouble in persuading the magistrates to remand Amy in custody, along with a large number of others. Whilst Amy was concerned, she was confident that she had done nothing to be worried about and took it all on the chin, but for April this was devastating. Loss and rejection again.

Whilst the legal process churned through protracted procedures, Amy was held first on remand and then in a deportation centre before returning to Australia by agreement. The police failed to prove a solid case against her, but equally she struggled to prove her innocence. Despite this, Amy was philosophical about the experience, as were her family, and determined not to let it derail her good intentions. She decided to study back home in Australia initially, before returning to her plans to travel across America whilst working for a large computer technology company. She did attempt to keep in touch with April through the occasional email, and held out the hope of meeting up again at some point.

For April, however, this was a defining moment. Having suffered so much; the violent loss of her virginity and her dignity, the premature death of her dear and only brother, her parents' separation and then the loss of her only real friend and support, at that stage was too much. The depth of despair was too great; the feelings of isolation, of being alone, of being overwhelmed were all too much. Shock, that sense of emotional numbness, physical and emotional exhaustion, all returned with a vengeance.

The project staff noticed the dramatic dip in April's mood and presentation. Their concerns were confirmed when finding her slumped in her room staring into open space.

Over the following few months, despite the project staff's genuine attempts to engage with her and limit the damage, April slipped over the edge into chaotic drug use and depression. Sadly, the draw of potential instant solutions from the unscrupulous pack of competing local drug dealers who plagued the women from the project proved to be a greater appeal than the offers of more intangible help from the project staff.

April resisted the project worker's advice to contact her parents, arguing that they had enough to deal with in their own lives at present without being burdened by this. Whilst that was true to an extent, both Mark and Jan would undoubtedly have responded positively to their daughter's plight had they known, but as far as they were concerned April was busily forging a new life for herself in London, didn't need them and wanted her independence.

Sadly this only added to their respective senses of isolation and pushed their relationships even further apart. April's condition deteriorated, she lost weight, often refused to eat and frequently withdrew into herself and into the relative comfort of the warmth and sanctuary of her room and her bed. Alone, trapped in her own destructive downward spiral of despair, she felt unable to break out.

The project staff continued to monitor her closely, with some success. At least self-imposed confinement to bed broke the circle of falling prey to the destructive pack of eagerly awaiting dealers looking to pedal their recipes of destruction for an easy profit.

In the weekly review meeting, April's case was discussed at length. The meeting was chaired as usual by the local manager who was responsible for four different projects in the area.

Her key worker outlined her circumstances, length of stay and current position, concluding that 'my heart goes out to this young woman. She's only eighteen and has gone through such a lot.'

'Yes, I'm sure we all agree,' replied the manager, 'but what structured support have we offered so far? Do we have a current medical opinion, for example?'

'No, not current; April refuses to go to see anyone.'

'Have we asked the GP to come here to see her?'

'No, not yet,' admitted her key worker.

'Have you contacted the police again, if as it seems the drug dealers are back on the patch?'

'Yes I've done that and they promised to intervene again to try to keep them at bay. None of the other girls have reported any problems in the last few weeks and we don't believe we have any of the residents dealing or using the heavy stuff at present.'

One of the more experienced staff who hadn't had direct dealings with April commented, 'From what you describe, it sounds to me like she's depressed, which clearly wouldn't be surprising after what she's gone through. Maybe we'd be better asking mental health to get involved, a community psychiatric nurse for example.'

'Have we any concerns about self-harm here, or suicide risk?' posed the manager. 'Are we in touch with her family?'

The discussion continued, including agonising over the ethical dilemma of whether April's condition warranted direct contact with her family despite April's wishes.

'No,' concluded the manager, 'I can't sanction that. She is an adult, after all. Right; some actions: send a request to the GP for a home visit; refer to Community Mental Health and monitor her food intake, mood and general presentation regularly over the next week and we'll review again then.'

Team members nodded and they moved on to discuss the next case.

The team proceeded to follow the actions set. The local GP did after some persuading agree to do a home visit. April was not particularly responsive and the GP's assessment was inconclusive.

'What did you make of her, doctor?' asked the duty officer.

'Obviously I can't disclose details, but she's very withdrawn at the moment and not in the right mind set to look beyond the immediate, but she's not suffering from any infection. I think you are right to contact the CPN and to monitor her closely. Have you had any reason to be concerned about suicide risk?' she asked.

'No, not directly, but April says very little nor shares her thoughts very often.'

'OK. Let's hope the CPN can break through the silence and engage with her. Tell them it must be a woman,' said the GP as she hurried off to her next call.

Despite the local community mental health services being overstretched and overwhelmed at times, Sally Wilson remained a committed and well motivated CPN. After a week of close monitoring by the project staff and an initial period away from the drugs, April was beginning to show some early signs of improvement. She was eating better and talking. The day before Sally came to visit, April had been outside for a short walk with two of the other residents and had enjoyed the relative fresh air and mild exercise.

It seemed that the project staff and the GP had judged it right, and when Sally arrived April was in a more amenable frame of mind and had agreed to talk to an empathic listener.

'Hello, April, I'm Sally. I've come to try to help you today. Is there somewhere we can talk privately?'

April lead her into an interview room.

'April, I'm not here to judge, or to tell you what to do; initially I'm just here to listen. I know something of your circumstances from the project staff, but you just tell me what you want to share and let's see if together we can start to make some sense of it,' said Sally calmly, with a warmth and a well practiced ability to put people at their ease.

'Sally, I just feel so alone; at times so desperate and I can't see a way out. I haven't got the energy to even think about it. Everything seems bad, negative, overwhelming,' explained April as she started to cry.

'OK, let those tears out, cry as much as you want to. Let the emotion go,' offered Sally reassuringly as she passed the box of tissues.

April felt able to talk openly for the first time since Amy was arrested and Sally listened attentively. They sat together actively engaged for over an hour before Sally tried to draw things to a conclusion and summarise what had been said.

'April, I think that's probably enough for now. Let's give you a chance to think about what you've said. Give yourself some credit for talking openly and don't punish yourself for struggling with your circumstances. What you have been through would rock the foundations of anyone – don't be surprised that you are finding it hard. Give it time and try to identify the positives. Take small steps. No need to set any timescales and be gentle with yourself.'

April smiled, and they parted with a warm embrace and agreed to meet again the following week. April did feel some relief in expressing her feelings and started to rediscover some energy; rediscover some hope.

Chapter Twenty-Four

April worked with Sally over the next few weeks and started to summon the energy and courage to think of at least ringing home to share her problems and reassure her parents. Sally helped her to clear away some debris from her mind and identify what was actually important to her. She was reminded of the strength she found during the trial, and with medication, support from the project and Sally's assistance, slowly started to feel some improvement. Over time she became more energised, began sleeping a more normal pattern and started engaging in activities during the day. All these things helped to create a sense of momentum and a sense of hope, which gradually replaced the feelings of despair. It felt like being released from self-imposed imprisonment from being trapped in a negative self-destructive spiral.

Sally helped by talking of others who had overcome trauma and not succumbed to despair but had learnt to manage it. She usefully described some case histories, mentioning some more high profile examples; Terry Waite, Brian Keegan and John McCarthy, all of whom had suffered deprivation in captivity but survived. She had talked about Ellen McArthur who had sailed around the world on her own overcoming sleep deprivation, raging seas, loneliness and ongoing repairs to triumph in the end. More recently Jessica Ennis who had showed such determination and coped with the public exposure as the face of the London games during the Olympics

2012 and managed to bring home the gold medal. April started reading some of these accounts and found them inspirational, and that they helped to reduce a sense of isolation and to restore her inner strength.

Steadily over the following few months April continued to make progress and to feel better. She had her bad days, but overall things were improving. The project staff became less concerned and relaxed their level of monitoring.

*

It was now several years since the incident and April was nearly nineteen. She was managing more consistently to keep negative thoughts and feelings at bay. She began to wonder what to do next, thinking that she couldn't stay at the project indefinitely, and was beginning to think about returning to education – to start to pick up the pieces, to start to take some control.

Perhaps it was now the right time to ring home, she thought.

Eventually, April chose a day when she felt that she was strong enough and picked up the phone to ring home. When the call was answered she felt an immediate sense of relief. Although the conversation was difficult and it was upsetting to hear that her parents remained separated, it felt good to hear her dad's voice. He at least was reassuring. Mark had been occupied with his own affairs although had remained concerned about his daughter but had felt it was best to leave her be for a while. April thought that he sounded clearly relieved to hear from her, as Mark tried not to make her feel guilty for not being in touch.

When April caught up with her mother, however, later that same day, she was far more dramatic and emotional. Jan could not help but release some of that pent up anxiety that had accumulated since April had left home. By the end of the conversation April felt emotionally drained.

*

Slowly bridges were built and after some consideration, April decided to take up her dad's offer to return home, initially to stay with him and then to look for something independent nearby. He had also offered to take her on holiday for a fortnight for some winter sun, rest and relaxation, before effectively starting the next stage of her life and trying to get back on track.

The holiday did them both good and Jan was OK about it and didn't attempt to be competitive or jealous.

Christmas was difficult without Sam and with all that had happened. It felt odd, more like three independent people who had happened to meet and decided to share Christmas together rather than being members of the same family.

April managed to find work. Initially back at the same shop where the manger still felt sorry for her, and then with a larger retail chain. Slowly her energy returned and she managed to resurrect some interest in the field of modern communication technology, and she wondered whether this was a likely direction for employment in the future. She saved her money, moved into independent accommodation and signed up to resume her education at the local college. April went on to complete her GCSEs and A levels over the following few years whilst continuing to work and to consider applying for university. She wasn't sure, however, what to study, quite where it might take her or what she wanted to do with her life. She still felt quite uncertain.

It had been hard returning to her home area and adjusting to Mum and Dad's separation. Most of her school friends had left, many to go to university. She had kept in touch with Lucy but didn't really feel part of that group anymore or that she had really established new friends or a new life. There were times when April felt that she was just surviving, drifting, but with little motivation, purpose or direction. She often just felt sad and sometimes still very angry.

Chapter Twenty-Five

It was shortly after her 22nd birthday that April received a letter from Australia. April immediately wondered, could it be from Amy?

Amy had kept in touch from time to time by email, but a letter was more personal and it was full of news. She had completed her commitments in America, returned to Australia and was about to get married! She wrote that her career was still going well and that she'd left the large corporate world and started her own business selling IT consultancy, support and web design to the industry that she had just left.

April read on, eagerly absorbing the good news. Whilst she was so pleased to hear of Amy's success, it compounded her sense of drift compared to Amy's strong sense of direction. Then as she read the last page there was both an invitation and an offer that she could hardly believe and that could change everything again. Amy had invited her to her wedding and sent an open invitation to go over to Australia, stay with her and help her to set up her new business. Wow! What an opportunity. April felt immediately excited. Why not, she thought, I've nothing to keep me here. She remembered the fondness and closeness that she felt she had with Amy at a time in her life when she desperately needed it. Call it fate, call it luck, but this seemed like a chance to break out – a chance of renewal. It was a potential lifeline and April immediately felt that she wanted to take it.

Both her mum and dad were more supportive and positive about the idea than April had expected. Indeed they both seemed so much more settled, and had established their own lives, yet still met regularly and did some things together. Privately, Jan felt some further sense of loss if April were to emigrate and Mark had reservations about how confident and resilient April may prove to be to take such a risk with a friend she had only known for a short time. Nevertheless he supported and encouraged her.

*

April did go to Australia. She worked with Amy and her new husband for two years, enjoying the carefree Australian outdoor life: the beach, the barbeques, the 'can do' attitude and the cosmopolitan East meets West culture. She developed her IT skills, her business knowledge and her confidence. She met some great people, and had several failed relationships before deciding it was time to move on again.

April still found trusting men very difficult, and feeling comfortable in a relationship and being at ease with sex without fear. She still had flashbacks taking her back to the horror of the whole affair, particularly the rapes. She struggled to feel anything other than anger about the impact the incident had on her family. She knew it didn't help, but nevertheless the anger was always there.

As Amy was about to have her first child, April returned to the UK to start a degree course at the University of Birmingham. She had decided to return to her scientific interest and to study for a degree in biology. She didn't feel up to the rigours of medicine and indeed whilst her GCSE and A level results had been good, they were not good enough to pursue that ambition. She thought that she would like to do some sort of work with people based on healing but wasn't sure yet what route that would take. It would also give her the opportunity to deal with her own demons in a more structured way.

It was whilst at university that she met Oliver. He too was a mature student, confident, self-assured and passionate. He saw something beautiful in April, and was enchanted and captivated by her. He courted her gently, made her feel wanted for who she was and allowed her time to overcome her fear and resistance to physical contact and learn to enjoy it. April found that she could trust him, found that she could take strength and pleasure in being with him, and in time found that she could love him.

Oliver was studying psychology and planned to work with children as an educational psychologist. He had a natural rapport with children and a love of life. He was never down, always positive and was kind and considerate. He was just what April needed. She was able to give him the love he craved and he reciprocated and understood her vulnerability.

April engaged in counselling over the period of her degree. She came to learn that anger and resentment were not helpful or constructive. She learned to talk through her anxieties and talk about the rapes, to release some of the hurt and the emotion, to heal, to recover. She had her moments of self-doubt, recurrence of bouts of depression and still felt some fear of re-victimisation – that somehow she was destined to suffer; that things would always go wrong for her; that she could be the victim of serious crime again.

*

Over time, love restored hope. Oliver and April graduated together and settled in Birmingham. Oliver achieved his ambition to become an educational psychologist and worked with children who were struggling with a variety of disorders and conditions. April went on to train as a physiotherapist and specialised in helping accident victims recover from their injuries. This gave her an outlet for her yearning to help others and make a positive contribution yet not risk getting too close to exposing her own vulnerabilities.

April and Oliver grew ever closer together. Their love and trust bound them to each other and helped April's healing. She went on to have two daughters, Olivia and September and a son, Harry.

Over the years that followed April often wondered what had become of the four men who dramatically intruded into her life. She wondered about their journey. She knew very little of the criminal justice system, so had no real idea of what might have happened to them. She still had a fear that if they were ever released they may come looking for her. She feared that they may blame her for their incarceration and that they could be seeking vengeance.

Nevertheless, as time passed April became stronger. Her bouts of depression became less severe and less frequent. The longer her experience of positive relationships became, the easier it was to place her previous experience in some context and to avoid cynicism and negativity. She grew to recognise that she also had the benefit of a relatively good start in life and therefore she had much positive early experience to draw on. She enjoyed the positive outcomes of seeing the patients she worked with recover and move on and could share those feelings with Oliver, who understood what it meant to her. He too took satisfaction from his work and they played off each other in sharing those good feelings. Their home was a warm and welcoming place; a place of nurture for the children; a place of hope and a place of joy.

*

It was some years later that April came to deal with a different patient. A human being with his own needs – a serious injury to recover from, but the difference was that the man attending her clinic was a serving prisoner.

Brad had grown up in poverty and deprivation, skipped school, got into crime and drugs at a very early age and become part of a notorious city gang. He lived on the streets practicing unimaginable degrees of inhumanity and depravity. He had learnt to subdue emotion. He had learnt to harm and he had learnt to hate. It was a pattern of armed robberies that had brought him into prison. Whilst in custody his criminal past had caught up with him and he had been subject to a revenge attack by other prisoners. He had been badly beaten and thrown down the stairs resulting in a broken hip, and he had also broken his leg in several places. He had been brought to the clinic for rehabilitation treatment and for help to recover. He needed to learn to walk again after several operations and months in and out of plaster.

April had experience of dealing with trauma victims and indeed she had dealt with a significant number of injured soldiers and was impressed with the ever improving developments in replacement limbs for amputees. These men, however, were soldiers who had served without question or regard for their own safety.

Generally they brought along camaraderie and a spirit that enhanced and encouraged recovery beyond survival. Not all, however. Sadly some did not recover physically or psychologically. How would she deal with a man who came from a very different background, a man who challenged her tolerance and humanity, a man who could derail her own sense of security? she wondered. Knowing her history, April's manager had at least taken the trouble to discuss it with her and despite her reservations had agreed to let April take part in Brad's treatment.

Brad was accompanied by a large, burly looking prison officer who clearly wasn't going to take any messing. April breathed deeply and although in some ways Brad's demeanour reminded her in part of the criminal gang that still haunted her, she was surprised by his pleasant disposition and polite and respectful manner.

Over the course of Brad's treatment he responded well and it proved to be helpful for April, too. Although painful, her contact with Brad did help in redressing some stereotypes and in helping to deal with some of her residual bad memories and fears.

It was following that experience that she saw an advert attempting to recruit prison visitors to offer support to long term prisoners in custody who had lost all family contact.

'What do you think of this, Oliver?' she asked over breakfast. 'The local prison is trying to recruit volunteers to support long term prisoners.'

'OK, I suppose they have their needs too, but who would want to do that?' he replied.

'I mean I might be interested, Oliver.'

Despite the obvious reservations, April had felt that some good had come out of her dealings with Brad and she was prepared to go that little bit further.

The recruitment and training process proved to be straight forward enough. She did, of course, declare her professional as well as personal interest, and she was approved to become a volunteer.

Chapter Twenty-Six

The years had not been easy for any of the gang members. Despite their early expectations custody had a way of grinding down resistance and sapping the will to maintain any hope of release.

Barry was never caught, but was always looking over his shoulder. Dog had spent years fighting the system, physically and legally. He had suffered periods of severe mental illness necessitating transfer back and forth between high security prison and hospital, earning him the nickname 'Mad Dog'. The prognosis for him was poor with little prospect of release. Charlie had died in custody from a heart attack after years of drug abuse.

After a bad start, Chaff, however, had made some progress. He had completed a wide range of courses aimed at changing his thinking and his outlook, accepting responsibility and learning to behave and act in a positive, responsible and constructive manner. He had done many hours of work on victim awareness, trying to acknowledge what he'd done and move towards some degree of understanding about what they had put the Hartwell family through and its likely impact. He often wondered what had happened to them. None of the Hartwell family had opted to work with the Victim Liaison Service at the time, and no direct contribution to the gang's sentence management had ever been received from them to be considered alongside other factors.

Both April and Chaff continued along their separate paths as the years rolled by. April enjoyed her role as a prison volunteer, both in helping the individual prisoners and also in helping her restore some faith in humanity and in people's capacity to change. She learnt about many of the common factors that linked offenders, and whilst that only provided a partial explanation, it did help her escape from some of her demons.

Given her experience, April was sometimes asked to explain to groups of prisoners something of her story as a victim. Although she found this incredibly hard, she also strangely took some strength in the often quite warm and even empathetic reaction of the groups she addressed. For many, although she had no connection with their own crime, hearing April talk had a powerful affect in bringing home the realities of the impact that crime can have on victims. It was not written down in a text book style, it was live, it was real and they could see, hear and feel her emotion as she told her story.

Research was encouraging about how this broad approach could help influence some offenders. Mediation, as it was referred to, was usually indirect; whilst the victim may have suffered the type of crime committed by the offender, they were not involved in the same actual incident, that being regarded in most cases as too much to expect the volunteers to endure. Prison staff discussed this approach with April openly. It would not work for all, it appealed to emotion, feelings and a sense of empathy, which some offenders simply didn't have or lacked in sufficient depth. For others it did appear to influence them and to help them along with other measures to reduce the risk of doing anything similar again, but like most approaches it was no panacea.

April worked with a few individuals to try to raise their awareness and insight into the likely impact of their criminal behaviour. This was often painful for both of them, but April was prepared to do it if she thought it helped. Ultimately it was about trying to ensure that others weren't left to endure what she had gone through.

Oliver encouraged her and could see that it was also part of her own recovery. They talked a lot about bitterness, anger and vengeance, and how those feelings, although perhaps justifiable, could ultimately be self-destructive. Notions of 'letting go' and 'moving on' were important barriers to cross in being able to deal with trauma and avoid seeing the world as an inherently threatening and dangerous place.

*

Over many years April continued to enjoy her work in rehabilitation as a physiotherapist, offering hope and recovery to many individuals from all backgrounds, both civilian and those from the armed services. She kept in touch with the local prison as a volunteer, giving the occasional talk and offering individual support to a selected prisoner, but this diminished in frequency over the years as she felt more confident that she had moved on from feeling that this was something she needed to do. She was also aware that with time the intensity of her experience diminished and therefore the power of the message she was able to deliver, coupled with a growing feeling as she got older that she had more than 'done her bit.'

The children all grew and developed into rounded, confident and independent young people, ready to face the world and find their own way. Oliver, for his part moved on from direct work with children back into the academic field and offered his experience, guidance and energy to new people coming into the service.

April often wondered what happened to those four men all those years ago – what had forged them, what drove and motivated them and where were they now.

A chance meeting with Kate, the police officer who had helped them through the trial, brought some of these feelings back to light. Kate was retired by now, but both of them were still involved in supporting victims of crime to some extent. They had met at a conference for volunteers helping various charities and were both really pleased to catch up. Kate was able to use her contacts to provide April with some basic information to satisfy her curiosity.

April decided that it was time to contact the Probation Victim Liaison Service to see if they could help her after all this time. She was warmed by their response. She learnt more about Chaff's progress and prospects. It helped her put her experiences into context as she concluded that some of the negative feelings would never leave her, but that there was no merit in bitterness or in maintaining anger any longer. She felt more resigned and in control at that moment than ever before. It really did feel to her that it was time to move on.

It was only a short time later that she heard again from the Probation Victim Liaison Service offering further intervention. After some further enquiries and suitable negotiation, arrangements were made for April to visit the open prison where Chaff was now held. It was felt that both were ready and willing to meet, albeit briefly, and that such an event could be beneficial to them both and indirectly be a service to the public in helping reduce and manage any risk that Chaff still posed.

An experienced mediator was present and Chaff was able to offer some explanation, an apology and explain something about what he had learnt over those intervening years. April listened, said that she was still affected by his actions, but that she had spent a lifetime trying often in vain to adapt and to prevail. She told him that she wished him no harm at this point just that he would harm no others. A statement of forgiveness was too much, but the spirit of reconciliation was implicit and powerful.

For April, although it wasn't said explicitly, she felt assured that if he was ever released he would no longer present a threat to her, and that was another major hurdle crossed.

April thought of Sam and of her parents. They had both adjusted in their own way and were pleased that she had spent some time with them before they died peacefully in their old age.

As she got up to leave the prison, April turned and said emphatically, 'If you ever call on someone unexpectedly again, be sure to knock the door first,' and she closed the door behind her and emerged into the light.

****

COMING SOON...

Green Terror

Chapter One

Cobra meeting, London

In a small, dark meeting room important matters were discussed; the very security of the nation, the balance of international diplomacy and the politics of pragmatism and compromise.

Towards the end of the meeting there was an interjection with new information.

'So, Nathan, what have we got?'

'This could be serious, Prime Minister,' replied his private secretary.

'Yes.'

'We have intelligence to suggest that the plane crash over South Africa last week wasn't due to chronic engine failure, but terrorist action, trying to embarrass the British Government over failure to make progress over certain international companies and unethical activity.'

'Yes, I see...and if your suspicion it right, would we be vulnerable?'

'Yes.'

'Um...' said the Prime Minister, considering his position.

'I'm afraid we live in a very uncertain world, Prime Minister.'

'Indeed.'

Oxford

Oxford, one of the world's most prestigious universities; a national treasure and institution. Many of the country's leaders had enjoyed their education in this hallowed place. What experience and contribution would this year's students make to the future of mankind and the development of civilisation?

Crichton marvelled at the sheer joy and splendour of the Oxford skyline, even on such a dull morning. Heading out from college towards the river he waved a hello to Arabella as he left Radcliffe Square. With the lessons of ancient history going through his mind and the ever present concern about the future of the planet, Crichton crossed the road into Christchurch Meadow, following the path to the boathouses. Rowing was a major preoccupation at Oxford, although not for Crichton for whom the privacy of the boathouse had more carnal implications.

Walking along the path by the river, he spoke to the usual range of people sitting on the benches; the old, the lonely, the relaxed and the stressed out, as the wading birds rushed to the water to avoid his purposeful steps. Crichton had his head full of ideas he wanted to share and discuss with Ahmed and Conrad. Conrad, he knew was always on time and probably had already settled into his first lunchtime pint in The Crown, their favourite pub by the river. Ahmed, he knew, however, was more unreliable and would probably be late as usual. Crichton approached the garden of The Crown with a sense of boyish excitement.

Crichton Broadhampton-Scott, attitudes and manners honed in the best of English public schools was relishing the academic challenge and pure indulgence of studying history and classics at Canterbury College Oxford, the college attended by both his father and grandfather and many members of his famous school.

Crichton was right that Conrad Lindstrand was already sitting comfortably in the garden overlooking the river. Educated in Sweden, Conrad always harboured an ambition to study abroad and was delighted to have been offered a place to study biology at Canterbury College. Environmental science was his major interest and he hoped to research climate change and its implication for global politics.

'Crichton, sit down. Let me get you a beer!'

'No, no, you've nearly finished yours; I'll get them in. The usual?'

As Crichton returned with two fresh real ales in hand, placed them on the table and the two young idealists smiled and shook hands.

'Conrad, have you been here long?'

'No, not really. I'm just thinking about presenting my paper this afternoon to the International Relations Society. It's about the case for radical action to avoid climatic catastrophe.'

'Really, how interesting! I feel so strongly about this, too. The mainstream and entrenched interests seem destined to ignore the growing weight of evidence that the world will soon be beyond the point of no return unless we act now! Conventional politics seems unable to deliver an answer; we need something more radical. What are we going to do?' said Crichton with conviction.

'Yes, I've been charting the likely impact of global temperature rise from 1-5 degrees centigrade and it's frightening.'

'Go on.'

'Well, the impact on food and water supplies, damage to eco systems, ever more erratic weather bringing flooding and major disruption could threaten our very cohesion and stability and lead to the breakdown of world order, leaving us to descend into chaos!'

'Chaos? Did I hear chaos on such a lovely day as this?' remarked Ahmed, as he approached with beer in hand. 'I assumed you two would have already started.'

'Indeed, the world won't wait for you, Ahmed!' replied Crichton.

Ahmed Salib, educated in Saudi Arabia and the USA, now studying PPE (politics, philosophy and economics). Calmly Ahmed sat down and joined the conversation, as sharp young minds addressed serious intractable great world problems with diligence and determination.

The three young men had soon bonded on arrival at Oxford and found solace in a common interest about the future of the planet. They had researched well and debated many times, usually coming to the same conclusion that the time for conventional approaches had past. A series of G8 conferences had produced lacklustre agreements over the years, which the signatories invariably failed to deliver. The Paris conference was heralded to be no different.

*